Edward Herbert of Cherbury, John C. Collin

**The Poems of Lord Herbert of Cherbury**

Edward Herbert of Cherbury, John C. Collin

**The Poems of Lord Herbert of Cherbury**

ISBN/EAN: 9783337406691

Printed in Europe, USA, Canada, Australia, Japan

Cover: Foto ©Andreas Hilbeck / pixelio.de

More available books at **www.hansebooks.com**

# POEMS OF LORD HERBERT.

THE

# POEMS OF LORD HERBERT

## OF CHERBURY

EDITED

WITH AN INTRODUCTION

BY

JOHN CHURTON COLLINS

LONDON

CHATTO AND WINDUS, PICCADILLY

1881

I INSCRIBE

THIS LITTLE VOLUME

TO MY FRIEND

WILLIAM BAPTISTE SCOONES,

AN

IMPERFECT EXPRESSION

OF

ESTEEM AND AFFECTION.

# PREFACE.

WHETHER the Poems, which are here for the first time prefented in a modern drefs, be of intrinfic value the reader will foon determine for himfelf. I have at leaft brought Herbert before the Court; and I have, I hope, fecured him a fair hearing. Henceforth he will not be condemned unheard.

With regard to the text, I have adhered with fcrupulous fidelity to that of the original edition; and I have collated the only two copies to which I could obtain accefs—the copy in the Britifh Mufeum, and the copy in the Bodleian Library at Oxford—without, however, difcovering any variety of readings. My principal difficulty has been with the punctuation, on which, of courfe, the fenfe of paffages frequently depends; and for this I have often had no guidance *from the original, which teems with palpable errors. The spelling has also been carefully revised, and though it has been for the most part modernised, I have thought it well to retain, in some cases, the older forms, so as to preserve the flavour of archaism. Obvious misprints have been silently corrected. In two passages only I have ventured to alter the text, and they both occur in 'The Idea.' In the seventh line the original reads 'bear,' which, as it makes no sense, and breaks the rhyme, I alter into 'bar.' Again, in the last line, 'whence' is substituted for 'when.' And for this reason. Herbert is alluding to the Platonic doctrine of ideas, and it is much more natural to suppose that he would speak of an idea* whence *the form began than of an idea* when *the form began. Though he is mistaken in supposing that the Platonic ideas admit of application to particular individuals, he was evidently acquainted with the 'Timæus' and with the 'Republic.'*

*J. CHURTON COLLINS.*

5 *King's Bench Walk, Temple.*

# CONTENTS.

## Contents. xi

# INTRODUCTION.

LORD HERBERT of Cherbury is one of the moſt intereſting, and in many reſpects one of the moſt eſſentially original characters, in our Literary Hiſtory. At once a philoſopher and a politician, a man of the world and a man of letters, it was his lot to flouriſh at a criſis of no ordinary importance in philoſophy, in politics, in literature. His youth was paſſed in the world of Hooker, Sydney, and Spenſer. Before he died Hobbes had written the *Elementa Philoſophica de Cive*, Barclay had publiſhed his *Argenis*, and Butler was collecting materials for *Hudibras*. He was a child of eight when Elizabeth addreſſed the ſoldiers at Tilbury Fort, and he lived to ſee Charles the Firſt betrayed by the Scots to the Engliſh Commiſſioners. He was the friend of Donne and Ben Jonſon; he was the correſpondent of Grotius and Gaſſendi. He thus ſtood midway between two great eras, moving in both. In temper he belonged to the era of the Renaiſſance, in intellect he belonged to the era of Des Cartes and Hobbes. His own ſervices to literature

were important.  His *De Veritate*, if it did not do much
for the advancement of metaphyfical philofophy, was the
work of a fearlefs, vigorous, and independent thinker ; a
work which exercifed confiderable influence on the pro-
grefs of Free Enquiry, and was the firft attempt made,
in this country at leaft, to reduce Deifm to a fyftem.
His *Life and Reign of Henry VIII.* is an admirable piece
of hiftorical compofition.  His *Expeditio Buckinghami
Ducis in Ream Infulam* is the beft account we have of
that unhappy adventure ; and his *Autobiography* is, if ever
autobiography was, a treafure for all time.

Thus interefting by his furroundings, thus important
in himfelf, we are the more attracted towards him becaufe
of the fulnefs with which we are acquainted with the
incidents of his perfonal hiftory.  We know him as we
know no other man of that age.  Never fince Jerome
Cardan laid bare for the world's infpection the innermoft
fecrets of his being, never fince Cellini told the ftory
of his ftrange viciffitudes, never fince Montaigne took
Europe into his confidence, had fuch a record as Herbert
has left us been committed to paper.  Whether he in-
tended his fingular confeffions for publication may well
be doubted.  He tells us himfelf that they were written
for the inftruction of his defcendents, and to enable
him to review his paft career, that he might reform
what was amifs if fuch reformation were poffible, that

he might comfort himfelf with the memory of whatever virtuous actions he might have done, and that he
might make his peace with God. In the courfe of this
review he not only narrates the adventures which he
had encountered on his way through life, but he enters
into minute particulars relating to his writings and
fpeculations—his ftruggles with his paffions, his ftruggles
with his reafon : he gives us his opinions on education, on
the conduct of life, on religion. And he is to all appearance unreferved. His frailties are not concealed, and
they are many ; but we feel that he has, on the whole,
gained rather than loft by a fcrutiny which few, indeed, of
our erring race could court with impunity. Nor is this
all. It is the portrait of a man with features eminently
ftriking and peculiar, whofe ways were never the ways of
common men, whofe thoughts were not the thoughts
either of his predeceffors or contemporaries. Nothing,
therefore, which Herbert has left us can be without importance ; for, whatever be its intrinfic value, it is the
product of an original mind developing itfelf under ex-
ceptionally interefting hiftorical conditions.

The world has long done juftice to his profe writings.
It is the object of the prefent volume to vindicate his
title to a place among Englifh poets. I have certainly no
wifh to be numbered among thofe gentlemen whofe in-
difcriminating induftry continues year after year to load

our libraries with treafures better hidden. I have no wifh to rob Oblivion of its legitimate prey. Some of Lord Herbert's poems are, I freely admit, not worth refufcitation, but many of them, or portions at leaft of many of them, feem to me authentic poetry. In almoft all of them we find originality and vigour, however fantaftic the conception, however rough the execution. But were their merits even lefs than they are, no cultivated man could regard them with indifference. The name of their writer would be a fufficient paffport to indulgent attention. We treafure the verfes of the authors of the *Nicomachæan Ethics*, and of the *Novum Organon*, though Ariftotle has no claim to a place among the Pleiad, or Bacon to a place befide Jonfon or Donne.

In my eftimate of Lord Herbert's poems I have hitherto ftood alone. His biographers and critics are unanimous in ignoring or condemning them. Antony Wood paffes them by without comment. Horace Walpole merely mentions them in his Catalogue of Herbert's Works. Neither Grainger nor the author of the life in the *Biographie Univerfelle* have anything to fay for them. Park, in a note on Walpole's *Life of Herbert*, coldly fpeaks of 'Lord Herbert's fcarce volume of metaphyfical love verfes, ingenious but unnatural, platonic in fentiment, but frequently grofs in expreffion, and marked by an eccentricity which pervaded the life and character of their

author;' and thefe remarks have been greedily copied into
fucceffive editions of bibliographic manuals, reprints, and
the like.   Ellis, in his *Specimens of Englifh Poetry*, is ftill
lefs favourable in his verdict, boldly obferving that young
Herbert 'fhowed more piety than tafte in publifhing his
father's poems.'   The author of an article on the *Autobiography* in the *Retrofpective Review* contents himfelf
with remarking that Lord Herbert is often 'both rugged
and obfcure in his verfes,' and 'was much more fitted to
wield the fword than the lyre.'   They have no place in
the *Selections* of Headley.   Even Campbell, who can
find a niche for Heminge and Picke, has no corner for
Herbert.   M. Charles de Rémufat, in his interefting and
valuable treatife, *Lord Herbert of Cherbury, fa Vie et
fes Œuvres*, expreffes fimilar opinions : 'Ses poéfies
anglaies, publiées par fon fecond fils, font d'un genre
moins ferieux '—(he has been fpeaking, and fpeaking de-
preciatingly, of Herbert's Latin poems)—' Quelques unes
font ingenieufes, la plufpart obfcures ; l'amour en eft le
fujet ordinaire, un amour platonique, exprimé cependant
avec plus de recherche que délicateffe.'   It is curious that
they fhould have efcaped the notice of Sir Egerton Brydges,
who has not, fo far as I can difcover, made any allufion
to them.   And this is the more remarkable, as he was
particularly interefted in the hiftory of the Herbert family,
and was the firft editor of the poems of William Herbert,

third Earl of Pembroke. When he obferved in the preface to his reprint of the Earl's poems that 'to fuffer them
to lie longer in oblivion would be to defraud an illuftrious
family of its greateft ornaments,' he made a remark which
would be far more applicable to the prefent volume.
Whatever opinion may be formed of Lord Herbert's
merits as a poet, there can be no queftion as to his
fuperiority to his kinfman.

It is ftrange that in his *Autobiography* Lord Herbert
makes no mention of his Poems, the exiftence of
which feems not to have been fufpected by any of
his diftinguifhed contemporaries. They were evidently
jotted down in moments of leifure, as occafion offered.
Some of them were the work of his youth, fome of his
middle age; the laft was written four years before his
death. This we gather from the dates prefixed to many
of them, the earlieft date being Auguft 1608, the lateft
October 1664. The biographers affure us that many of
thefe poems had appeared in print during Herbert's lifetime, and are to be found in the poetical collections of
the period. For thefe collections I have fearched in vain.
I doubt, I muft own, the truth of the ftatement, and fufpect
that it has been loofely copied, without any attempt to
afcertain its correctnefs, from Antony Wood; and I am
the more inclined to believe this becaufe they have faithfully
repeated one grofs blunder of Wood's—a blunder which

would at once have been rectified by confulting the work to which Wood refers. It is this, and it is fignificant : In the third volume of his *Athenæ Oxonienfes* (edition Blifs, p. 242) Wood fays : ' Other of Lord Herbert's poems I have feen in the books of other authors occafionally written, particularly in that of Jofhua Sylvefter, entitled *Lacrymæ Lacrymarum,* 1613.' This affertion is repeated by Walpole, by Sir Walter Scott in the Prefatory Memoir to Lord Herbert's *Autobiography,* publifhed at Edinburgh in 1809, by the editor of Murray's reprint of the *Life,* and by all the bibliographers. Now there is not a line of Lord Herbert's to be found in Sylvefter's work. What Wood was thinking of was no doubt the *Elegy for the Prince* (fee Poems, page 33), which certainly was publifhed during Herbert's lifetime, but which appeared, not in Sylvefter's *Lacrymæ Lacrymarum,* but in a collection entitled *Sundry Funeral Elegies on the Untimely Death of the Moft Excellent Prince Henry,* compofed by feveral hands, 1613. However this may be, the poems made their appearance in a collected form in 1665, nearly feventeen years after Herbert's death ; and were, as we learn from the Preface, given to the world by Henry Herbert, his youngeft fon. Of thefe poems there appears to have been only one edition. The volume is now extremely rare ; indeed, it is one of the rareft known to bibliographers.

The reader will at once difcover that Herbert belongs, like his brother, to that fchool of poets whofe characteriftics have been fo admirably analyfed by Johnfon—the Metaphyfical or Phantaftic School. This fingular fect firft appeared during the latter years of Elizabeth's reign. Their origin is popularly afcribed to Dr. Donne, though it would in truth be more correct to fay that in the poetry of Donne their peculiarities of fentiment and expreffion are moft confpicuoufly illuftrated. They owed their origin, indeed, not to the influence of Donne, but to the fpirit of the age. In all eras of great creative energy poetry paffes neceffarily through two ftages : in the firft ftage, imagination predominates ; in the fecond, reflection. In the firft ftage, men feel more than they think ; in the fecond, they think more than they feel. If a literature run its natural courfe, we may predict with abfolute certainty that mere rhetoric will ufurp the place of the eloquent language of the paffions, that fancy will be fubftituted for imagination, and that there will ceafe to be any neceffary correfpondence between the emotions and the intellect. This ftage was not completely attained till the age of Cowley. In the poetry of Donne we find the tranfition between the two ftages marked with fingular precifion. Some of his poems remind us of the richeft and frefheft work of the Elizabethan age ; in many of them he out-Cowleys Cowley himfelf. But his work was not the work, in any fenfe, of a creator. He contributed no new elements, either to thought or to diction. What he did was to unite the vicious peculiarities of others, to indulge habitually in what they indulged in only occafionally. He was not, for example, the firft to fubftitute philofophical reflection for poetic feeling, as his contemporaries, Samuel Daniel, Sir John Davies, and Fulke Greville, were fimultaneoufly engaged in doing the fame thing. He was not the firft to indulge in abufe of wit, in fanciful fpeculations, in extravagant imagery, or in grotefque eccentricities of expreffion. But, in addition to uniting thefe vices, he carried them further than any of his predeceffors or contemporaries had done, and, aided by the fpirit of the age, he fucceeded in making them popular. It would not, perhaps, be faying too much to fay that no fingle author contributed more to the foundation of the Metaphyfical School than Jofhua Sylvefter, whofe tranflation of Du Bartas preceded the ' metaphyfical' poems of Donne, and was probably as favourite a work with Donne as it certainly was with moft of the young poets of that age. The ftyle of Donne is, however, marked by certain diftinctive peculiarities which no intelligent critic would be likely to miftake, and his influence on contemporary poetry was unqueftionably confiderable. Lord Herbert appears to have been the earlieft of his difciples. Indeed, moft of the poems in Herbert's collection in which the influence of Donne is moſt perceptible, had been written, as the dates ſhow, long before the poems of Donne were given to the world. But he was, we know, perſonally acquainted with Donne, and Donne, like many of the poets of that age, was in the habit of circulating copies of his poems among private friends.\* His acquaintance with his maſter commenced, no doubt, while he was ſtill a ſtudent at Univerſity College; for we learn from Walton's *Life of George Herbert* that when Mrs. Herbert was living with her ſon Edward at Oxford Donne arrived there on a viſit, and became, during her reſidence at Oxford, one of her moſt valued friends and adviſers. His beautiful poem entitled the *Autumnal* was written in honour of Mrs. Herbert. As Herbert was then a youth of eighteen, and Donne a man of upwards of forty, it is not unreaſonable to ſuppoſe that Donne aſſiſted both in moulding the youth's taſtes and in directing his ſtudies.

Where Herbert moſt reminds us of Donne is not

---

\* Dr. Groſart, in his laborious and inſtructive account of Donne and his writings, tells us that ſeveral of Donne's deſcriptive and ſatirical poems were in circulation among friends certainly before 1614, and that ſome of his lyrics were in circulation before 1613. (See his remarks on his edition of Donne, vol. ii., *Eſſay on the Life and Writings of Donne*, pp. xxxi. and xxxii.)

fo much in his lyrics as in his poems written in the heroic meafures; in the two fatires, for example, in the verfes 'To his Miftrefs for her True Picture,' in the elegy on Donne himfelf. The poem alfo entitled 'The Idea' is very much in his friend's vein, as well as written in a meafure which Donne perhaps invented, and which was certainly a favourite with him. The numerous poems dedicated to the praife of dark beauty were perhaps fuggefted by Donne's verfes *To a Lady of Dark Complexion.* In the two poems on Platonic Love we may alfo difcern the prefence of the mafter. It would, of courfe, be abfurd to affert that the lyric poetry of Donne had no influence on that of Herbert, but its influence was far lefs confiderable than it would at firft fight appear to be. Herbert's rhythm is his own. Where it is mufical its mufic is not the mufic of the older poet, where its note is harfh and diffonant it is no echo of the difcords of that unequal and moft capricious finger. Many of Donne's favourite meafures he has not employed; fome of his own meafures, the meafures in which he has been moft fuccefsful, have no prototype in Donne's poems. What he owes in lyric poetry to the leader of the Metaphyfical School is to be found, fo far as form is concerned, rather in what Donne fuggefted than in what he directly taught. In fpirit he owed, it muft be allowed, much. From Donne he learned to fport with extravagant fancies, to

fubftitute the language of the fchools for the language
of the heart, to think like the author of the *Enneads*
and to write like the author of *Euphues.* He has, however, had the good tafte to avoid the groffer faults of his
mafter. He never indulges in prepofterous abfurdities;
he never, if we except one couplet, clothes myfticifm
in motley.

Herbert's poems are of too mifcellaneous a character
to be exactly claffified. They may be roughly divided into
Sonnets, Elegies, Epitaphs, Satires, Mifcellaneous Lyrics,
and Occafional Pieces. However unequal thefe com-
pofitions may be in point of execution, there are two
things which the reader of Herbert may, in the more
ambitious poems at leaft, generally promife himfelf—originality and vigour. The Sonnets need not detain us
long. The one 'To his Watch' (page 1) is well expreffed.
The ftyle is in happy unifon with the fentiment, and the
final claufe is folemn and impreffive. The laft verfe of
the fonnet 'To her Face' (page 6),

'Sure Adam finn'd not in that fpotlefs face,'

though fomewhat obfcure, is a really fine line. In the
fonnet written near Merlou Caftle (page 12), the couplet
defcribing the groves on the banks of the ftream,

'Embroidering through each glade
An airy filver and a funny gold,'

prove that Herbert had the eye of a poet. The moſt
ſtriking of them is the addreſs 'To Black Itſelf' (page 59),
which is particularly intereſting, becauſe it contains the
germ of part at leaſt of the idea which was afterwards
ſo magnificently embodied by Blanco White in his famous
ſonnet. White was moſt likely immediately indebted to
Sir Thomas Browne, but Browne was no doubt well
acquainted with Herbert and his writings. With regard
to his Elegies—I am not, of courſe, including among
them the lyric elegy on page 49—I ſhall perhaps conſult
his fame beſt by paſſing them by without comment.
Two or three verſes in the ' Elegy on the Prince' will no
doubt pleaſe and ſtrike, but there praiſe muſt end, even
from an editor. Of the Epitaphs, the moſt original is the
' Epitaph upon Himſelf' (page 81), the moſt groteſque that
on Cecilia Boulfer (page 29), the moſt eloquent and
pleaſing that on William Herbert of Swanſey (page 31).
The two ſatires are of very unequal merit. The ſecond,
page 20, would diſgrace Taylor the Water Poet. The
firſt, ' The State Progreſs of Ill,' though intolerably harſh
and barbarous in ſtyle, contains ſome intereſting remarks.
Of the Occaſional Pieces, thoſe which moſt nearly re-
ſembled the poems of which we have been ſpeaking are
the verſes entitled ' To her Mind ' (page 8), and ' To his
Miſtreſs for her True Picture' (page 74), both being in the
heroic couplet, and both being in the ſame contemplative

vein. To thofe who are fond of tracing refemblances between the works of men of genius who are feparated by many years from each other, it will be interefting to obferve how clofely Herbert fometimes reminds us of Mr. Browning. In the verfes, for example, ' To her Mind,' there is a paffage which might excufably be miftaken for the work of the great philofophical poet of our day :—

> ' Thus ends my Love, but this doth grieve me moft
> That fo it ends ; but that ends too; this yet,
> Befide the wifhes, hopes and time I loft,
> Troubles my mind awhile, that I am fet
> Free, worfe than deny'd : I can neither boaft
> Choice nor fuccefs, as my cafe is, nor get
> Pardon from myfelf, that I loved not
> A better miftrefs, or her worfe. This debt
> Only 's her due, ftill that fhe be forgot
> Ere chang'd, left I love none ; this done, the taint
> Of foul inconftancy is cleared at leaft
> In me ; there only refts but to unpaint
> Her form in my mind, that fo difpoffeff'd,
> It be a temple, but without a faint.'

— the fame elliptical mode of expreffion, the fame intermixture of fentiment and logic, the fame curious refinements of fpeculative meditation. The verfes ' To his Miftrefs for her True Picture ' will not find, and they certainly do not deferve, many admirers. It may be queftioned whether Platonifm has ever clothed itfelf in fuch grotefque language as in the laft couplet of this ftrange poem:

> ' Hear from my body's prifon this my call,
> Who from my mouth-grate and eye-window bawl.'

The lyric pieces are of very unequal merit. But in making out a cafe for Herbert my bufinefs is only with his beft work; and if we judge him by his beft work, he is certainly entitled to no mean place among the lyrifts of the Metaphyfical School. His mufic is, it muft be owned, full of difcords—his verfes will fometimes not even fcan, and yet he poffeffed not only a fine ear for rhythmic effect, but his rhythm is of great compafs and variety. Occafionally his verfe has a weight, a fullnefs and dignity, not unworthy of Dryden; for example, two ftanzas like thefe (pages 10 and 11):

> ' Nay, thou art greater, too! More deftiny
>    Depends on thee than on her influence.
>    No hair thy fatal hand doth now difpenfe
> But to fome one a thread of life muft be.

> \*     \*     \*     \*     \*

> ' But ftay! methinks new beauties do arife
>    While fhe withdraws thefe glories which were fpread.
>    Wonder of Beauties! fet thy radiant head,
> And ftrike out Day from thy yet fairer eyes.'

Nor can we refufe the gift of lyric melody to the writer of a ftanza like this :—

> ' Then think each minute that you lofe a day.
> The longeft youth is fhort,
> The fhorteft age is long : Time flies away,
> And makes us but his fport,
> And that which is not Youth's is Age's prey.'

Or to the writer of fuch poems as we find on page 56, and on page 46.

But Herbert's greateft metrical triumph is that he was the firft to difcover the harmony of that ftanza with which the moft celebrated poet of our own day has familiarifed us. The glory of having invented it belongs indeed to another, but the glory of having paffed it almoft perfe᧣ into Mr. Tennyfon's hands belongs unqueftionably to Herbert. And it is due alfo to Herbert to fay that he not only revealed its fweetnefs and beauty, but that he anticipated fome of its moft exquifite effe᧣s and variations. Take, for example, the following ftanza, where the paufe occurs at the end of the fecond line :—

> ' For where affe᧣ion once is fhown,
> No longer can the World beguile ;
> Who fees his penance all the while
> He holds a torch to make her known.'—*Ditty*, page 42.

Or thefe lines, where the paufe is made at the end of the firft line :—

> ' Elfe fhould our fouls in vain elect,
>     And vainer yet were Heaven's laws
>     When to an everlafting caufe
>     They give a perifhing effect.'—Page 96.

Or again :—

> ' Nay, I proteft ; though Death with his
>     Worft counfel fhould divide us here ;'—Page 94.

where the paufe occurs at the end of the fourth fyllable. An analytical examination of the metre of *In Memoriam* will fhow that on alternations and interchanges of thofe paufes the poet has not only relied for varying his harmony, but for producing fome of his moft pleafing effects. Indeed, in Herbert's two poems we find anticipated the exact cadence, the exact note of the modern poet. I queftion, for example, whether the niceft ear could distinguifh lines like thefe from the Laureate's :—

> ' Were not our fouls immortal made,
>     Our equal loves can make them fuch.'

> ' As one another's myftery,
>     Each fhall be both, yet both but one.'

> ' Who fees his penance all the while
>     He holds a torch to make her known.'

Other points of refemblance, into which there is no

neceffity for entering here, can fcarcely fail to fuggeft themfelves to thoughtful readers. It is curious that we fhould be able to point—and to point, I venture to think, without at all ftraining analogy—to two poems of this forgotten poet which recall fo exactly the work of the author of *In Memoriam* and the work of the author of *Sordello*. If the circumftance prove little elfe, it proves at leaft the verfatility of Herbert's powers.

The beft of Herbert's lyrics is the poem of which we have juft been fpeaking — the 'Ode upon a Queftion moved whether Love fhould Continue for Ever.' It is a little prolix, and it is occafionally obfcure; but the fineft ftanzas in it are exquifitely beautiful. Next would come, in the eftimation of many perhaps, the verfes 'Upon combing her Hair' (page 10), which are fingularly vigorous and picturefque. We feel, however, that their founding rhetoric is fomewhat out of place—the ftyle is too elevated for the theme, a common fault with poets of the fecond order. Among other lyrics of a ferious caft the 'Elegy over a Tomb' (page 49) and the verfes 'To her Hair' (page 56) deferve mention. Of the lighter lyrics the 'Ditty in Imitation of the Spanifh' will probably be read with much pleafure. The Platonic Love poems, though not without intereft and even merit, cannot be faid to hold a very high rank among poems of the clafs to which they belong. With one exception—the ode on page 92, to which I have already referred—they are little calculated either to pleafe or to ftrike. They have all the frigidity and pedantic ingenuity of Petrarch and Bembo without thofe beauties of expreffion which ftill attract us in the Sonnetti and Canzoni. ' The Idea ' is, however, well worth attentive perufal. Rarely have the doctrines of pure Platonifm been more fkilfully applied, rarely have philofophy and fentiment been more ingenioufly blended.

Herbert's moft confpicuous defects, both in thefe and in his other poems, are want of finifh and exceffive obfcurity. He feldom does juftice to his conceptions. He had evidently no love for the labour of the file, and he has paid, like Donne and Fulke Greville, the juft penalty for his careleffnefs.

The Latin poems of Herbert are fcarcely likely to find favour in the eyes of modern fcholars. Their diction is, as a rule, involved and obfcure ; they teem with forced and unclaffical expreffions. His hendecafyllabics are intolerably harfh, and violate almoft every metrical canon. His Elegiacs are not more fuccefsful; indeed, the only tolerable copy among the poemata are the verfes on a Dial, for the epigrams are below contempt. In his hexameters he fucceeds better. The ' Menfa Luforia ' is ingenious and not inelegant, and the ' Pro Laureato Poetâ,' though unneceffarily obfcure, is, like the epiftle to Guftavus, extremely fpirited. But even at his beft he cannot for an inſtant be compared with his contemporaries, Owen, Milton, Cowley, or May, who wrote Latin, nor indeed with the purity of the poets of the Italian Renaiſſance, but with wonderful fluency and vigour. Beſide the Latin poems appearing in this volume, Herbert was the author of three others, entitled reſpectively 'Hæredibus ac Nepotibus ſuis Præcepta,' which is in elegiacs, 'De Vitâ Humanâ Philoſophica Diſquiſitio,' and 'De Vitâ Cœleſti ex ejuſdem principiis Conjeƈtura,' which are in hexameters. They are to be found among certain traƈts appended to the _De Cauſis Errorum_, printed in 1645.* The two laſt appear alſo in the _Autobiography_, and they are by far the beſt. But as theſe poems are not likely to intereſt readers in our day, and poſſeſs little or no value in themſelves, we have refrained from adding them, even by way of appendix, to the preſent volume.

---

* The exaƈt title of the volume is, _De Cauſis Errorum, una cum traƈtatu De Religione Laici et Appendice ad Saccrdotes, necnon quibuſdam poematibus._ _Londini_, 1645 (Walpole ſays, erroneouſly, 1647).

# OCCASIONAL

# VERSES

OF

# EDWARD LORD HERBERT

## BARON

OF

## CHERBURY AND CASTLE-ISLAND.

*Deceafed in Auguſt* 1648.

LONDON:

*Printed by* T. R. *for* THOMAS DRING,

*At* THE GEORGE *in* FLEET STREET, *near* CLIFFORD'S INN.

1665.

## To the
## RIGHT HON. EDWARD LORD HERBERT,
### BARON OF CHERBERY IN ENGLAND AND
### CASTLE ISLAND IN IRELAND.

*My Lord,*

*This Collection of some of the scattered Copies of Verses, composed in various and perplexed times, by Edward Lord Herbert, your late Grandfather, belongs of double right to your Lordship, as Heir and Executor; and had it been in his power to have bequeathed his Learning by Will, as his Library and Personal Estate, it may be presumed he would have given it to you as the best Legacy. But Learning being not of our Gift, though of our Acquisition, nor of the Parapharnalia of a Lady's Chamber, nor of the casual and fortunate Goods of the World, it must be acknowledged of a transcendency beyond natural things, and a beam of the Divinity. For by the Powers of Knowledge Men are not only diftinguiſhed from Men, but carried above the reach of ordinary Perſons, to give Reaſons even of their Belief—not that men believe becauſe they know, but know becauſe they believe. Faith muſt precede Knowledge ; and yet men are not bound to accept matters of Religion, though Religion be the objeƈ and employment of faith, not of reaſoning merely without Reaſon and probable Inducements.*

*That the learned Centuries are paſt, and Learning in declenſion, is too great a truth, which may introduce Atheiſme with Ignorance ; for as Ignorance is the Mother of Devotion amongſt the Papiſts, ſo 'tis the Mother of Atheiſme amongſt the Ignorant.*

*The great and moſt dangerous deſign of our Church and National Enemies, is to make us out of Love with Learning, as a Mechanick thing and beneath the Spirits of the Nobility and of Princes : whereas nothing improves and enlightens the underſtandings of great Perſons but Learning, and not only ennobles them far above their birth, but enables them to impoſe on others, and to give rather than take advice. The Learned, Generous, and Vertuous Perſon needs no*

*Anceſtors. And what can ſo properly be call'd ours as what is of our purchaſe?*

'Gentiles agunt ſub nomine Chriſtiano' *was an old Reproach upon the Primitive Chriſtians; and now Men out-act the Gentiles.*

*The Goods of this life are all Hydropick,* Quo plus bibuntur, plus ſitiuntur. *Men are the drier for drinking and the poorer for covetouſneſs: no ſatiety, no fulneſs, but in ſpiritual things. The way of Vertue appeared to the Heathen to be the only way to Happineſs, and yet they knew not many vertues which are the Glory of Chriſtianity, as Humility, Denying of our ſelves, Taking up the Croſs, forgiving and loving our Enemies, which the Heathen took for follies rather than Vertues.*

*As for Poetry, it bears date before Proſe, and was of ſo great authority with the common People and the wiſer ſort of antiquity, that it was in veneration with their Sacred Writ and Records, from which they derived their divinity and belief concerning their Gods, and that their Poets, as Orpheus, Linus, and Muſæus, were deſcended of the Gods, and divinely inſpired, from the extra-*

*ordinary Motions of their Minds, and from the Relations of strange Visions, Raptures, and Apparitions.*

    *My Lord, excuse the liberty of this Dedication, and believe me,*

*Your Lordship's Uncle*

*and Humble Servant,*

*HENRY HERBERT.*

*March* 18*th*, 166$\frac{4}{5}$.

# OCCASIONAL VERSES.

## *TO HIS WATCH*
### *WHEN HE COULD NOT SLEEP.*

UNCESSANT Minutes, whilſt you move you tell
    The time that tells our life, which, though it run
Never ſo faſt or far, your new begun
Short ſteps ſhall overtake ; for though life well

May ſcape his own Account, it ſhall not yours.
    You are Death's Auditors, that both divide
And ſum what ere that life inſpir'd endures
    Paſt a beginning, and through you we bide

The doom of Fate, whoſe unrecall'd Decree
    You date, bring, execute ; making what's new
    Ill, and good old, for as we die in you,
You die in Time, Time in Eternity.

## DITTY.

**D**EEP Sighs, Records of my unpitied Grief,
    Memorials of my true though hopelefs Love,
Keep time with my fad thoughts, till wifh'd Relief
My long defpairs for vain and cauflefs prove.
Yet if fuch hap never to you befall,
I give you leave, break time, break heart, and all.

Lord, thus I fin, repent, and fin again,
As if Repentance only were in me
Leave for new Sin; thus do I entertain
My fhort time, and Thy Grace, abufing Thee
And Thy long fuffering, which, though it be
Ne'er overcome by Sin, yet were in vain
If tempted oft: thus we our Errors fee

Before our Punifhment, and fo remain
Without Excufe: and, Lord, in them 'tis true
Thy Laws are juft; but why doft Thou diftrain
Ought elfe for life fave life? That is Thy due,
The reft Thou mak'ft us owe, and may'ft to us
As well forgive. But, oh! my fins renew,
Whilft I do talk with my Creator thus.

## A DESCRIPTION.

\*I SING her worth and praifes, I,
  Of whom a Poet cannot lie.
The little World the Great fhall blaze,
Sea, Earth, her Body; Heaven, her Face,
Her Hair, Sunbeams, whofe every part
Lightens, inflames each Lover's Heart,
That thus you prove the †Axiom true,
Whilft the Sun helped Nature in you.
Her Front, the white and azure fky
In Light and Glory raifed high,
Being o'recaft by a cloudy frown,
All Hearts and Eyes dejecteth down;
Her each Brow, a celeftial Bow
Which through this Sky her Light doth fhow,
Which doubled, if it ftrange appear
The Sun's likewife is doubled there;
Her either Cheek, a blufhing Morn,
Which, on the Wings of Beauty born,
Doth never fet, but only fair
Shineth exalted in her hair;

---

\* μικρύκοσμος μακροκόσμος.    † *Sol et homo generant hominem.*

3

Within her Mouth Heaven's Heav'n reſide ;
Her words the ſouls there Glorifi'd ;
Her Noſe, th'Æquator of this Globe,
Where Nakedneſs, Beauty's beſt Robe,
Preſents a form all Hearts to win.
Laſt Nature made that Dainty Chin,
Which that it might in every faſhion
Anſwer the reſt, a Conſtellation
Like to a Deſk, She there did place
To write the Wonders of her Face.
In this Cœleſtial Frontiſpiece,
Where Happineſs eternal lies,
Firſt arranged ſtand three Senſes,—
This Heaven's Intelligences,
Whoſe ſeveral Motions ſweet combined
Come from the firſt Mover, her Mind.
The weight of this Harmonique Sphere
The Atlas of her Neck doth bear,
Whoſe favours Day to Us imparts
When Frowns make Night in Lovers' Hearts.
Two foaming Billows are her Breaſts,
That carry raiſ'd upon their Creſts
The Tyrian Fiſh : More white's their Foam
Then that whence Venus once did come.
Here take her by the Hand, my Muſe,
With that Sweet Foe, to make my Truce,

To compact Manna beſt compar'd,
Whoſe dewy inſide's not full hard.
Her Waiſt's an everſ'd Pyramis
Upon whoſe Cone Love's Trophy is.
Her Belly is that Magazine
At whoſe peep Nature did reſigne
That precious Mould by which alone
There can be framed ſuch a One :
At th' entrance of which hidden Treaſure,
Happy making above meaſſure,
Two Alabaſter Pillars ſtand,
To warn all paſſage from that Land,
At foot whereof engraved is
The ſad *Non Ultra* of Man's Bliſs.
The back of this moſt pretious Frame
Holds up in Majeſty the Same ;
Where to make Muſic to all Hearts
Love bound the deſcant of her parts.
Though all this Beauty's Temple be
There's known within no Deity
Save Virtues ſhrin'd within her Will.
As I began, ſo ſay I ſtill,
I ſing her Worth and Praiſes, I,
Of whom a Poet cannot lie.

## *TO HER FACE.*

FATAL Afpect! that haft an influence
        More powerful far than thofe Immortal Fires
That but incline the Will and move the Senfe
Which thou alone conftrainft, kindling defires
Of fuch a holy force, as more infpires
The Soul with Knowledge, than Experience
Or Revelation can do with all
Their borrow'd helps : Sacred Aftonifhment
Sits on thy Brow, threat'ning a fudden fall
To all thofe Thoughts that are not lowly fent
In wonder and amaze, dazzling that Eye
Which on thofe Myfteries doth rudely gaze.
Vow'd only unto Love's Divinity :
Sure Adam finn'd not in that fpotlefs Face.

## TO HER BODY.

R EGARDFUL Prefence ! whofe fix'd Majefty
　　Darts Admiration on the gazing Look
That brings it not : State fits enthron'd in thee,
Divulging forth her Laws in the fair Book
Of thy Commandëments, which none miftook
That ever humbly came therein to fee
Their own unworthinefs. Oh, how can I
Enough admire that Symmetry, expreft
In new Proportions, which doth give the Lie
To that Arithmetic which hath profeft
All Numbers to be Hers ? Thy Harmony
Comes from the Spheres, and there doth prove
Strange meafures, fo well grac'd, as Majefty
Itfelf like thee would reft, like thee would move.

## TO HER MIND.

EXALTED Mind! Whofe character doth bear
    The firft idea of Perfection, whence
Adam's came, and ftands fo.  How can'ft appear
In words that only tell what here-
Tofore hath been ?  Thou need'ft as deep a fenfe
As Prophecy, fince there's no difference
In telling what thou art and what fhalt be.
Then pardon me that Rapture do profefs
At thy outfide, that want for what I fee
Defcription of.  Here amaz'd I ceafe
Thus——
Yet grant one queftion and no more, crav'd under
Thy gracious leave : How, if thou wouldft exprefs
Thyfelf to us, thou fhouldft be ftill a wonder ?

Thus ends my Love, but this doth grieve me moft
That fo it ends ; but that ends too ; this yet,
Befides the Wifhes, hopes, and time I loft,
Troubles my mind awhile, that I am fet

Free, worſe than denied : I can neither boaſt
Choice nor Succeſs as my Caſé is, nor get
Pardon from myſelf, that I loved not
A better Miſtreſs, or her worſe.   This Debt
Only's her due, ſtill that ſhe be forgot
Ere chang'd, left I love none : this done, the taint
Of foul Inconſtancy is clear'd at leaſt.
In me, there only reſts but to unpaint
Her form in my mind, that ſo diſpoſſeſt,
It be a Temple, but without a Saint.

## UPON COMBING HER HAIR.

BREAKING from under that thy cloudy Veil
Open and fhine yet more ; fhine out more clear,
Thou glorious golden-beam-darting hair,
Even till my wonder-ftricken Senfes fail.

Shoot out in light, and fhine thofe Rays on far,
Thou much more fair than is the Queen of Love,
When fhe doth comb her in her Sphere above,
And from a Planet turns a Blazing Star.

Nay, thou art greater, too !   More deftiny
Depends on thee than on her influence.
No hair thy fatal hand doth now difpenfe,
But to fome one a thred of life muft be.

While gracious unto me thou both doft funder
Thofe glories which, if they united were,
Might have amazed fenfe, and fhew'ft each hair
Which, if alone, had been too great a wonder.

And now fpread in their goodly length, fh'appears
No creature which the earth might call her own ;
But rather one that, in her gliding down,
Heav'ns beams did crown, to fhew us fhe was theirs.

And come from thence, how can they fear Time's rage,
Which in his power elfe on earth moft ftrange,
Such golden treafure doth to Silver change
By that improper Alchemy of Age ?

But ftay ! methinks new Beauties do arife
While fhe withdraws thefe Glories which were fpread :
Wonder of Beauties ! fet thy radiant head,
And ftrike out Day from thy yet fairer eyes.

## *DITTY IN IMITATION OF THE SPANISH*
## *ENTRE TANTOQUE EL'AVRIL.*

NOW that the April of your youth adorns
  The garden of your face,
Now that for you each knowing Lover mourns,
  And all feek to your grace,
Do not repay affection with fcorns.

What though you may a matchlefs Beauty vaunt,
  And all that Hearts can move
By such a power that feemeth to enchant,
  Yet, without help of Love,
Beauty no pleafure to itfelf can grant.

Then think each minute that you lofe a day.
  The longeft youth is fhort,
The fhorteft Age is long; Time flies away,
  And makes us but his fport,
And that which is not Youth's is Age's prey.

See but the braveſt Horſe that prideth moſt,
   Though he eſcaped the War,
Either from Maſter to the Man, is loſt,
   Or turned unto the Car ;
Or elſe muſt die with being ridden Poſt.

Then loſe not Beauty, Lovers, Time, and all,
   Too late your fault you ſee,
When that in vain you would theſe days recall.
   Nor can you virtuous be,
When without theſe you have not wherewithal.

## THE STATE-PROGRESS OF ILL.

I SAY, 'tis hard to write Satires. Though Ill
   Great'ned in his long courſe, and ſwelling ſtill,
Be now like to a Deluge, yet, as Nile,
'Tis doubtful in his original. This while
We may thus much on either part preſume,
That what ſo univerſal are, muſt come
From cauſes great and far. Now in this State
Of things, which is leaſt like good, Men hate,
Since 'twill be the leſs ſin. I do ſee
Some ill required, that one poiſon might free
The other; ſo ſtates, to their Greatneſs, find
No faults required but their own, and bind
The reſt. And though this be myſterious, ſtill,
Why ſhould we not imagine how this Ill
Did come at firſt, how't keeps his greatneſs here,
When 'tis diſguiſ'd, and when it doth appear.
This Ill, having ſome attributes of God
As to have made it ſelf and bear the rod
Of all our puniſhments, as it ſeems, came

Into the World to rule it, and to tame
The pride of Goodneſs ; and though his Reign
Great in the hearts of men he doth maintain
By love, not right, he yet the tyrant here
(Though it be him we love and God we fear),
Pretence yet wants not, that it was before
Some part of Godhead, as Mercy, that ſtore
For Souls grown Bankrupt, their firſt ſtock of Grace,
And that which the ſinner of the laſt place
Shall number out, unleſs th' Higheſt will ſhow
Some power not yet reveal'd to Man below.

But that I may proceed, and ſo go on
To trace Ill in his firſt progreſſion,
And through his Secret'ſt ways, and where that he
Had left his nakedneſs as well as we,
And did appear himſelf,

　　I note that in　　　　　　　　 ⎧ 　　　　 ⎫ Peccamus nobis.
The yet infant world how ⎨ Gradus mali funt quo. ⎬
　　Miſchief and ſin,　　　　　　 ⎩ 　　　　 ⎭ Nocemus aliis.

His Agents here on earth, and eaſy known,
Are now concealed Intelligencers grown :
For ſince that as a Guard th' Higheſt at once
Put Fear t' attend their private actions,
And Shame their publick, other means being fail'd,
Miſchief under doing of Good was veil'd,

15

And Sin, of Pleafure; though in this difguife
They only hide themfelves from mortal eyes.
Sins, thofe that both com- and o-mitted be,
Once hot and cold, but in a third degree
Are now fuch poifons, that though they may lurk
In fecret parts awhile, yet they will work
Though after death; nor ever come alone,
But fudden-fruitful multiply ere done.
While in this monftrous birth they only die
Whom we confefs, thofe live which we deny.
Mifchiefs, like fatal Conftellations,
Appear unto the ignorant at once
In glory and in hurt, while th'unfeen part
Of the great caufe may be perchance the Art
Of th' Ill and hiding it, which that I may
Ev'n in his firft original difplay,
And beft example, fure amongft Kings, he,
Who firft wanted fucceffions to be,
A Tyrant was, wife enough to have chofe
An honeft man for King, which fhould difpofe
Thofe beafts, which being fo tame, yet otherwife
As it feems, could not herd; And with advife
Somewhat indifferent for both, he might
Yet have provided for their Children's right,
If they grew wifer, not his own, that fo
They might repent, yet under treafon, who

16

Ne'er promif'd faith : though now we cannot fpare
(And not be worfe) Kings, on thofe terms, they are
No worfe than we could fpare (and have been fav'd)
Original fin.  So then thofe Priefts that rav'd
And prophefy'd, they did a kind of good
They knew not of, by whom the choice firft ftood.
    Since, then, we may confider now as fit
State government, and all the Acts of it,
That we may know them yet, let us fee how
They were derived, done, and are maintained now,
That Princes may by this yet underftand
Why we obey as well as they command.
State a proportion'd colour'd table is,
Nobility the mafter-piece in this,
Serves to fhew diftances ; while being put
'Twixt fight and vaftnefs they feem higher, but
As they're further off; yet as thofe blue hills
Which th'utmoft border of a Region fills,
They are great and worfe parts, while in the fteep
Of this great Profpective they feem to keep
Further abfent from thofe below, though this
Exalted Spirit, that's fure a free Soul, is
A greater Privilege than to be born
At Venice, although he feek not rule, doth fcorn
Subjection, but as he is flefh, and fo
He is to dulnefs, fhame, and many moe

Such properties, knows, but the Painter's Art,
All in the frame is equal.   That deſert
Is a more living thing, and doth obey
As he gives poor, for God's ſake (though they
And Kings aſk it not ſo), thinks Honours are
Figures compoſ'd of lines irregular,
And happy-high knows no election
Raiſeth man to true Greatneſs but his own.
Meanwhile ſugar'd Divines, next place to this,
Tell us Humility and Patience is
The way to Heaven, and that we muſt there
Look for our Kingdom ; that the great'ſt rule here
Is for to rule ourſelves.   And that they might
Say this the better, they to no place have right
B'inheritance, while whom Ambition ſways,
Their office is to turn it other ways.
   Thoſe yet, whoſe harder minds Religion
Cannot invade, nor turn from thinking on
A preſent greatneſs, that combin'd curſe of Law
Of officers' and Neighbours' ſpite doth draw
Within ſuch whirlpools, that till they be drown'd
They ne'er get out, but only ſwim them round.
   Thus brief, ſince that the infinite of ill
Is neither eaſie told nor ſafe, I will
But only note how freeborn Man, ſubdu'd
By his own choice, that was at firſt endu'd

With equal power over all, doth now ſubmit
That infinite of Number, Spirit, Wit,
To ſome eight Monarchs.   Then why wonder Men
        Their rule of horſes ?
The world, as in the Ark of Noah, reſts
Compoſ'd as then, few Men and many Beaſts.


*Aug.* 1608.
*At Merlou in France.*

## SATYRA SECUNDA

### OF TRAVELLERS FROM PARIS.

BEN JOHNSON, travel is a second birth
Unto the Children of another Earth ;
Only as our King Richard was, so they appear,
New born to another World, with teeth and hair.
While got by Englifh Parents, carried in
Some Womb of thirty-tun and lightly twin,
They are delivered at Calais or at Dieppe,
And ftrangely ftand, go feed themfelves, nay, keep
Their own money ftreightways ; but that is all,
For none can underftand them when they call
For anything.   No more than Badger,
That call'd the Queen Monfieur, laid a wager
With the King of his Dogs who underftood
Them all alike, which Badger thought was good.
But that I may proceed.   Since their birth is
Only a kind of Metempfychofis,
Such Knowledge as their Memory could give
They have for help, what time thefe Souls do live
In Englifh clothes ; a body which again

They never rife unto, but, as you fee
When they come home, like children yet that be
Of their own bringing up ; all they learn is
Toys and the Language, but to attain this
You muft conceive they're cofen'd, mocked, and come
To Fourbourgs St. Germans, there take a Room
Lightly about th' Ambaffadors, and where,
Having no Church, they come Sundays to hear
An invitation which they have moft part,
If their outfide but promife a defert,
To fit above the Secretaries' place,
Although it be almoft as rare a cafe
To fee Englifh well cloth'd here, as with you
At London, Indians.   But that your view
May comprehend at once them gone for Blois
Or Orleans ; learn'd French, now no more Boys
But perfeft men at Paris, putting on
Some forc'd difguife, or labour'd fafhion,
To appear ftrange at home, befides their ftay,
Laugh and look on with me, to fee what they
Are now become ; but that the poorer fort,
A fubjeft not fit for my Mufe nor fport,
May pafs untouch'd, let's but confider what
Elpus is now become, once young, handfome, and that
Was fuch a Wit, as very well with four
Of the fix might have made one, and no more,

Had he been at their Valentine, and could
Agree, your Rus fhould ufe the ftock who would
Carefully in that, ev'n as 'twere his own
Put out their Jefts, briefly one that was grown
Ripe to another tafte than that wherein
He is now feafoned and dry'd, as in
His face by this you fee, which would perplex
A ftranger to define his years, or fex ;
To which his wrinkles, when he fpeaks doth give
That Age his words fhould have, while he doth ftrive,
As if fuch births had never come from brain
To fhew his mots deliver'd without pain,
Nor without After-throes. Sometimes as grace
Did overflow in circles o're his face,
Ev'n to the brim, which he thinks fure
If this pofture do but fo long endure
That it be fix'd by Age he'll look as like
A fpeaking fign, as our St. George to ftrike,
That, where he is, none but will hold their peace
If th' have but the leaft good manners, or confefs,
If he fhould fpeak, he did prefume too far
In fpeaking then, when others readier are.
Now that he fpeaks are complemental fpeeches
That never go off but below the breeches
Of him he doth falute, while he doth wring
And with fome loofe French words which he doth
  ftring,     22

Windeth about the arms, the legs and fides,
Moft ferpent-like of any man that bides
His indirect approach, which being done
Almoft without an introduction,
If he have heard but any bragging French
Boaft of the favor of fome noble wench,
He'll fwear 'twas he did her graces poffefs,
And damn his own foul for the wickednefs
Of other men, ftrangeft of all in that.
But I am weary to defcribe you what,
Ere this, you can.   As for the little fry
That all along the ftreet turn up the eye
At everything they meet, that have not yet
Seen that fwol'n vicious Queen Margaret,
Who were a monfter ev'n without her fin,
Nor the Italian comedies wherein
Women play Boys.——I ceafe to write.
To end this Satire and bid thee good Night.

*Sept.* 1608.

I MUST depart, but like to his laſt breath
   That leaves the ſeat of life for liberty,
I go, but dying, and in this our death
Where ſoul and ſoul is parted, it is I
      The deader part yet fly away,
         While ſhe, alas ! in whom before
         I liv'd, dies her own death and more,
      I feeling mine too much, and her own ſtay.
But ſince I muſt depart, and that our love
Springing at firſt but in an earthly mould
Tranſplanted to our ſouls, now doth remove
Earthly affects, which time and diſtance would,
      Nothing now can our loves allay,
         Though as the better Spirits will
         That both love us and know our ill,
      We do not either all the good we may.
Thus when our Souls that muſt immortal be,
      For our loves cannot die, nor we (unleſs
We die not both together) ſhall be free
      Unto their open and eternal peace.
Sleep, Death's Embaſſador, and beſt
      Image, doth yours often ſo ſhow,
      That I thereby muſt plainly know,
Death unto us muſt be freedom and reſt.

*May* 1608.

## MADRIGAL.

HOW ſhould I love my beſt?
What though my love unto that height be grown,
That taking joy in you alone,
I utterly this world deteſt.
Should I not love it yet as th' only place,
Where Beauty hath his perfect grace,
And is poſſeſt?

But I beauties deſpiſe.
You, univerſal beauty ſeem to me,
Giving and ſhewing form and degree
To all the reſt, in your fair eyes.
Yet ſhould I not love them as parts whereon
Your beauty, their perfection,
And top doth riſe?

But ev'n my ſelf I hate.
So far my love is from the leaſt delight,
That at my very ſelf I ſpite.
Senſeleſs of any happy ſtate,
Yet may I not with juſteſt reaſon fear,
How hating hers, I truly her
Can celebrate?

# Madrigal.

Thus unrefolved ftill,
Although world, life, nay what is fair befide,
I cannot for your fake abide,
Methinks I love not to my fill.
Yet, if a greater love you can devife,
In loving you fome otherwife,
Believe't I will.

## ANOTHER.

DEAR, when I did from you remove,
　　I left my joy, but not my love;
　　　　That never can depart.
It neither higher can afcend,
　　Nor lower bend.
Fixt in the centre of my heart,
　　As in his place,
And lodged fo, how can it change,
　　Or you grow ftrange?
Thofe are earth's properties and bafe.
Each where, as the bodies divine,
　　Heav'n's lights and you to me will fhine.

## TO HIS FRIEND BEN JOHNSON, OF HIS
## HORACE MADE ENGLISH.

IT was not enough Ben Johnſon to be thought
    Of Engliſh Poets beſt, but to have brought
In greater ſtate to their acquaintance one
So equal to himſelf and thee, that none
Might be thy ſecond, while thy Glory is
To be the Horace of our times and his.

## EPITAPH. CÆCIL-BOULFER

### QUÆ POST LANGUESCENTEM MORBUM
### NON SINE INQUIETUDINE
### SPIRITUS &c. CONSCIENTIÆ OBIIT.

Intelligitur
de figurâ
mortis
præfigendâ.

METHINKS Death like one laughing lies,
　　Shewing his teeth, fhutting his eyes,
Only thus to have found her here
He did with fo much reafon fear,
　　And fhe defpife.

For barring all the gates of Sin,
Death's open ways to enter in,
She was with a ftrict fiege befet,
So what by force he could not get,
　　By time to win.

This mighty Warrior was deceived yet,
For what he mutin * in her powers, thought
　　Was but their zeal;
And what by their excefs might have been wrought,
　　Her fafts did heal.

---

* Mutiny.

Till that her noble foul, by thefe, as wings,
Tranfcending the low pitch of earthly things,
As being reliev'd by God and fet at large,
And grown by this, worthy a higher charge,
Triumphing over Death to Heaven fled,
And did not die, but left her body dead.

*July* 1609.

## EPITAPH. GULI. HERBERT DE SWANSEY
### QUI SINE PROLE OBIIT AUG. 1609.

GREAT Spirit, that in New Ambition,
    Stoop'd not below his merit,
But with his proper worth being carry'd on,
Stoop'd at no fecond place, till now in one
    He doth all place inherit.

Live endlefs here in fuch brave memory,
    The beft tongue cannot fpot it ;
While they which knew, or but have heard of thee,
Muft never hope thy like again to be,
    Since thou haft not begot it.

## IN A GLASS WINDOW FOR INCONSTANCY.

L OVE, of this cleareſt, fraileſt glaſs,
  Divide the properties, ſo as
In the diviſion may appear
Clearneſs for me, frailty for her.

## ELEGY FOR THE PRINCE.*

MUST he be ever dead ?   Cannot we add
     Another life unto that Prince that had
Our fouls laid up in him ?   Could not our love,
Now when he left us, make that body move
After his death one Age ?   And keep unite
That frame wherein our fouls did fo delight ?
For what are fouls but love ? fince they do know
Only for it, and can no further go.
Senfe is the Soul of Beafts, becaufe none can
Proceed fo far as t'underftand like man.
And if Souls be more where they love than where
They animate, why did it not appear
In keeping him alive ?   Or how is fate
Equal to us, when one man's private hate
May ruin Kingdoms, when he will expofe
Himfelf to certain death, and yet all thofe
Not keep alive this Prince, who now is gone,
Whofe loves would give thoufands of lives for one ?
Do we then die in him, only as we
May in the world's harmonique body fee
An univerfally diffufed foul

---

* Henry, Prince of Wales.   He died in November, 1612.

Move in the parts which moves not in the whole?
So though we reft with him, we do appear
To live and ftir awhile, as if he were
Still quickening us?   Or do (perchance) we live
And know it not?   See we not Autumn give
Back to the earth again what it received
In th' early Spring?   And may not we deceived
Think that thofe powers are dead, which do but fleep,
And the world's foul doth reunited keep?
And though this Autumn gave what never more
Any Spring can unto the world reftore,
May we not be deceived, and think we know
Ourfelves for dead?   Becaufe that we are fo
Unto each other, when as yet we live
A life his love and memory doth give,
Who was our world's foul, and to whom we are
So reunite, that in him we repair
All other our affections ill beftowed :
Since by this love we now have fuch abode
With him in Heaven as we had here, before
He left us dead.   Nor fhall we queftion more
Whether the Soul of Man be memory
As Plato thought : * We and pofterity

* It would be interefting to know where Plato has made
this fingular affertion.   I fear it is more eafy to account for
Herbert's remark than to corroborate it.

Shall celebrate his name, and virtuous grow
Only in memory that he was fo,
And on thofe terms we may feem yet to live,
Becaufe he lived once, though we fhall ftrive
To figh away this feeming life fo faft,
As if with us 'twere not already paft.
We then are dead, for what doth now remain
To pleafe us more, or what can we call pain
Now we have loft him ?   And what elfe doth make
Difference in life and death, but to partake
Nor Joy nor Pain ?   Oh death ! could'ft not fulfil
Thy rage againft us no way but to kill
This Prince in whom we liv'd ? that fo we all
Might perifh by thy hand at once, and fall
Under his ruin ?   Thenceforth though we fhould
Do all the actions that the living would,
Yet we fhall not remember that we live,
No more than when our mother's womb did give
That life we felt not.   Or fhould we proceed
To fuch a wonder, that the dead fhould breed,
It fhould be wrought to keep that memory
Which being his, can, therefore, never die.

*November* 9, 1612.

## EPITAPH OF KING JAMES.

HERE lies King James, who did fo propagate
    Unto the World that bleft and quiet ftate
Wherein his fubjects liv'd, he feemed to give
That peace which Chrift did leave; and did fo live,
As once that King and Shepherd of his Sheep,
That whom God faved, here he feemed to keep,
Till with that innocent and fingle heart
With which he firft was crown'd he did depart,
To better life. Great Brittain, fo lament
That Strangers more than thou may yet refent
The fad effects, and while they feel the harm
They muft endure from the victorious arm
Of our King Charles, may they fo long complain,
That tears in them force thee to weep again.

## A VISION.

### A LADY COMBING HER HAIR.

WITHIN an open curled fea of gold       The hair.
    A Bark of Ivory one day I faw,      The comb.
Which ftriking with his oars did feem to draw    The teeth of
Tow'rds a fair Coaft which I then did behold.    the comb.
                                                      Her fide.

A Lady held the Stern, while her white hand,
    Whiter than either ivory or sail,      The cuff or
                                                        fmock fleeve.
    Over the furging waves did fo prevail
That fhe had now approached near the land.    Her fhoulder.

When fuddenly, as if fhe feared fome wrack,
    And yet the Sky was fair, and Air was clear,
    And neither Rock, nor Monfter did appear    Wart.
Doubling the Point, which fpied, fhe turned back.

Then with a fecond courfe I faw her fteer,    Combing in an-
                                                      other place.
    As if fhe meant to reach fome other Bay,
    Where being approached, fhe likewife turned away,
Though in the Bark fome waves now entred were.   Hairs in the
                                                      comb.

Though varying oft her courſe at laſt I found,
  While I in queſt of the Adventure go,

**She had given over combing.**  The Sail took down and Oars had ceas'd to row,
And that the Bark itſelf was run aground.

**Her face.**  Wherewith Earth's faireſt creature I beheld,

**Her hair put up and comb caſt away.**  For which both Bark and Sea I gladly loſt.

  Let no Philoſopher, of Knowledge boaſt,
Unleſs that he my Viſion can unfold.

TEARS flow no more, or if you needs muſt flow,
  Fall yet more ſlow,
 Do not the world invade.
From ſmaller ſprings than yours rivers have grown,
  And they again a Sea have made
Brackiſh like you, and which like you hath flown.

Ebb to my heart, and on the burning fires
  Of my deſires
 Let your torrents fall.
From ſmaller Sparks than theirs ſuch ſparks ariſe
  As into flame converting all,
This world might be but my love's ſacrifice.

Yet if, the tempeſts of my ſighs, so slow
  You both muſt flow,
 And my deſires ſtill burn,
Since that in vain all help my love requires,
  Why may not yet their rages turn
To dry thoſe tears and to blow out thoſe fires ?

*Italy,* 1614.

# DITTY

### TO THE TUNE OF A CHE DEL QUANTO MIO OF PESARINO.

WHERE now fhall thefe accents go ?
   At which creatures filent grow
While Woods and Rocks do fpeak,
   And feem to break
Complains too long for them to hear,
Saying I call in vain : *Echo*—All in vain.
    : = :     : = :     : = :
Where there is no relief : *Ec.*—Here is no relief.

Ah why then fhould I fear
Unto her rocky heart to fpeak that grief
In whofe laments thefe bear a part ?
     Then, cruel heart,
    Do but fome anfwer give.
I do but crave. = Do you forbid to live or bid to
   live ?
    *Echo*—Live.

## DITTY.

CAN I then live to draw that breath
  Which muſt bid farewell to thee?
Yet how ſhould death not ſeize on me?
Since abſence from the life I hold ſo dear muſt
  needs be death.

While I do feel in parting
  Such a living dying,
As in this my moſt fatal hour,
  Grief ſuch a life doth lend
As quick'ned by his power
  Even death cannot end.

I am the firſt that ever lov'd,
  He yet that for the place contends,
  Againſt true love ſo much offends
That even this way it is prov'd.

For whofe affeétion once is fhown,
  No longer can the World beguile;
  Who fees his penance all the while,
He holds a Torch to make her known.

You are the firft were ever lov'd,
  And who may think this not fo true,
  So little knows of love or you,
It need not otherwife be prov'd.

For though the more judicious eyes
  May know when Diamonds are right,
  There is required a greater light
Their eftimate and worth to prize.

While they who moft for beauty ftrive
  Can with no Art fo lovely grow,
  As fhe who doth but only owe
So much as true affeétions give.

Thus firft of Lovers I appear,
  For more appearance makes me none,
  And thus are you belov'd alone,
That are priz'd infinitely dear.

Yet, as in our Northern Clime,
  Rare fruits, though late, appear at laſt;
  As we may fee fome years being paſt,
Our Orange trees grow ripe with time.

So think not ſtrange, if Love to break
  His wonted Silence now makes bold;
  For a Love is feven years old,
Is it not time to learn to fpeak?

Then gather in that, which doth grow
  And ripen to that faireſt hand.
  'Tis not enough that trees do ſtand
If their fruit fall and periſh too.

## EPITAPH OF A STINKING POET.

HERE ſtinks a Poet I confeſs,
  Yet wanting breath ſtinks ſo much leſs.

## *A DITTY TO THE TUNE OF COSE FERITE,*

### *MADE BY LORENZO ALLEGRE TO ONE SLEEPING. To be sung.*

*A*H *Wonder!*
   So fair a heaven,
   So fair, &c.

And no Star shining.
Ay me and no Star, &c.
'Tis paſt my divining.

   *Yet ſtay!*
May not perchance this be ſome riſing Morn
   Which in the ſcorn
Of our World's light diſcloſes
This air of violets, that ſky of roſes ?

   *'Tis ſo!*
An oriental ſphere
Doth open and appear,
   Aſcending bright;
Then ſince thy hymen I chant
May'ſt thou new pleaſures grant,
   Admired light.

## EPITAPH
## ON SIR EDWARD SACKVILLE'S CHILD,
### WHO DIED IN HIS BIRTH.

R EADER ! here lies a child that never cried,
  And therefore never died.
  'Twas neither old nor yong,
Born to this and the other world in one.
  Let us then ceaſe to moan,
Nothing that ever died hath liv'd ſo long.

## KISSING.

COME hither, Womankind, and all their worth,
   Give me thy kiſſes as I call them forth;
Give me thy billing kiſs; that of the Dove,
      A Kiſs of Love;
The Melting Kiſs, a Kiſs that doth conſume
      To a perfume;
The extract Kiſs, of every ſweet a part;
      A Kiſs of Art;
The Kiſs which ever ſtirs ſome new delight,
      A Kiſs of Might;
The twacking ſmacking Kiſs, and when you ceaſe,
      A Kiſs of Peace;
The Muſick Kiſs, crotchet and quaver time;
      The Kiſs of Rhyme;
The Kiſs of Eloquence which doth belong
      Unto the tongue;
The Kiſs of all the Sciences in one,
      The Kiſs alone.
So 'tis enough.

## DITTY.

IF you refuſe me once, and think again,
      I will complain.
You are deceived ; Love is no work of Art,
    It muſt be got and born,
      Not made and worn,
Or ſuch wherein you have no part.

Or do you think they more than once can die
      Whom you deny ?
Who tell you of a thouſand deaths a day,
    Like the old Poets feign,
      And tell the pain
They met but in the common way ?

Or do you think it is too ſoon to yield
      And quit the Field ?
You are deceived, they yield who firſt intreat.
    Once one may crave for love,
      But more would prove
This heart too little, that too great.

Give me then fo much love, that we may burn
      Paſt all return,
Who midſt your beauties, flames, and spirit live,
      So great a light muſt find
      As to be blind
To all but what their fires give.

Then give me fo much love, as in one point,
      Fixed and conjoint,
May make us equal in our flames arife,
      As we ſhall never ſtart,
      Until we dart
Lightning upon the envious eyes.

Then give me fo much love, that we may move
      Like ſtars of love,
And glad and happy times to Lovers bring,
      While glorious in one ſphere
      We ſtill appear
And keep an everlaſting ſpring.

## ELEGY OVER A TOMB.

MUST I then fee, alas! eternal night
    Sitting upon thofe faireft eyes,
And clofing all thofe beams, which once did rife
    So radiant and bright,
That light and heat in them to us did prove
    Knowledge and Love?

Oh, if you did delight no more to ftay
    Upon this low and earthly ftage,
But rather chofe an endlefs heritage,
    Tell us at leaft, we pray,
Where all the beauties that thofe afhes ow'd
    Are now beftow'd?

Doth the Sun now his light with yours renew?
    Have Waves the curling of your hair?
Did you reftore unto the Sky and Air
    The red and white and blue?
Have you vouchfafed to flowers fince your death,
    That fweeteft breath?

Had not Heav'n's Lights elfe in their houfes flept,
    Or to fome private life retir'd ?
Muft not the Sky and Air have elfe confpir'd
    And in their Regions wept ?
Muft not each flower elfe the earth could breed
    Have been a weed ?

But thus enrich'd may we not yield fome caufe
    Why they themfelves lament no more,
That muft have changed courfe they held before,
    And broke their proper Laws,
Had not your Beauties giv'n their fecond birth
    To Heaven and Earth ?

Tell us, for Oracles muft ftill afcend
    For thofe that crave them at your tomb ;
Tell us, where are thofe Beauties now become
    And what they now intend ;
Tell us, alas ! that cannot tell our grief,
    Or hope relief.

1617.

## EPITAPH ON SIR FRANCIS VERE.

R EADER,—
       If thou appear
   Before that tomb attention give,
       And do not fear,
       Unlefs it be to live,
   For dead is great Sir Francis Vere.

Of whom this might be faid, Should God ordain
   One to deftroy all finners whom That One
   Redeem'd not there, that fo He might atone
His chofen flock, and take from earth that ftain
   That fpots it ftill, he worthy were alone
   To finifh it, and have, when they were gone,
This world for him made Paradife again.

## TO MRS. DIANA CECYLL.

DIANA CECYLL, that rare beauty thou doſt
      ſhow
    Is not of Milk, or Snow,
  Or ſuch as pale and whitely things do owe,
But an illuſtrious Oriental Bright,
  Like to the Diamond's refracted light,
Or early Morning breaking from the Night.

Nor are thy hair and eyes made of that ruddy beam
    Or golden-ſanded ſtream
  Which we find ſtill the vulgar Poet's theme,
But reverend black, and ſuch as you would ſay
Light did but ſerve it, and did ſhew the way
By which at firſt night did precede the day.

Nor is that ſymmetry of parts and form divine
    Made of one vulgar line,
  Or ſuch as any know how to define,
But of proportions new, ſo well expreſt
That the perfections in each part confeſt
Are beauties to themſelves and to the reſt.

## To Mrs. Diana Cecyll.

Wonder of all thy Sex ! let none henceforth inquire
　　Why they fo much admire,　　　‑
　　Since they that know thee beft afcend no higher.
Only be not with common praifes wooed,
Since admiration were no longer good,
When men might hope more then they underftood.

†

## TO HER EYES.

B LACK eyes, if you feem dark,
   It is becaufe your beams are deep
   And with your foul united keep.
   Who could difcern
Enough into them there, might learn
   Whence they derive that mark,
   And how their power is fuch
That all the wonders which proceed from thence,
Affecting more the mind then fenfe,
      Are not fo much
The works of light, as influence.

      As you then joined are
Unto the foul, fo it again
By its connexion doth pertain
      To that firft caufe,
Who, giving all their proper Laws,
      By you doth beft declare
      How he at firft being hid

Within the veil of an eternal night,
Did frame for us a fecond light,
    And after bid
It ferve for ordinary fight.

    His image then you are;
If there be any yet who doubt
What power it is that doth look out
    Through that your black,
He will not an example lack,
    If he fuppofe that there
    Were grey or hazel Glafs,
And that through them, though sight or soul
    might fhine,
He muft yet at the laft define
    That beams which pafs
Through black, cannot but be divine.

## TO HER HAIR.

BLACK beamy hairs, which fo feem to arife
From the extraction of thofe eyes,
That unto you fhe deftin-like doth fpin
The beams fhe fpares, what time her foul retires,
 And by thofe hallowed fires
 Keeps houfe all night within.

Since from within her awful front you fhine, -
 As threads of life which fhe doth twine,
And thence afcending with the fatal rays
To crown thofe temples, where Love's wonders
  wrought,
 We afterwards fee brought
 To vulgar light and praife.

Lighten through all your regions, till we find
 The caufes why we are grown blind,
That when we fhould your Glories comprehend,
Our fight recoils, and turneth back again,
 And doth, as 'twere in vain,
 Itfelf to you extend.

## To her Hair.

Is it, becaufe paft black, there is not found
    A fix'd or horizontal bound ?
And fo as it doth terminate the white,
It may be faid all colours to infold,
      And in that kind to hold
      Somewhat of infinite ?

Or is it that the centre of our fight,
    Being veiled in its proper night,
Difcerns your blacknefs by fome other fenfe
Than that by which it doth pied colours fee,
      Which only therefore be
      Known by their difference ?

Tell us, when on her front in curls you lie,
    So diaper'd from that black eye,
That your reflected forms may make us know
That fhining light in darknefs all would find,
      Were they not upward blind
      With the Sun-beams below.

## SONNET OF BLACK BEAUTY.

**B**LACK beauty, which above that common light,
    Whofe Power can no colors here renew
  But thofe which darknefs can again fubdue,
Doft ftill remain unvary'd to the light?

And like an object equal to the view,
    And neither chang'd with day nor hid with night,
    When all thefe colours which the world call bright,
And which old Poetry doth fo purfue,

Are with the night fo perifhed and gone,
    That of their being there remains no mark,
Thou ftill abideft fo entirely one,
    That we may know thy blacknefs is a fpark
Of light inacceffible, and alone
    Our darknefs which can make us think it dark.

## ANOTHER SONNET TO BLACK IT SELF.

THOU Black wherein all colours are compof'd,
    And unto which they all at laft return;
Thou colour of the Sun where it both burn,
And fhadow, where it cools; in thee is clof'd
Whatever nature can, or hath difpof'd
    In any other here; from thee do rife
Thofe tempers and complexions which difclof'd
    As parts of thee, do work as myfteries
Of that thy hidden power; when thou doft reign
    The characters of fate fhine in the Skies,
And tell us what the Heavens do ordain :
    But when Earth's common light fhines to our eyes
Thou fo retir'ft thyfelf, that thy difdain
    All revelation unto man denies.

59

## THE FIRST MEETING.

A S fometimes with a Sable Cloud
        We fee the Heavns bow'd,
    And darkning all the fire,
Until the lab'ring fires they do contain
        Break forth again ;
Ev'n fo from under your black hair
    I faw fuch an unufual blaze
Lightning and fparkling from your eyes,
And with unufed prodigies
    Forcing fuch amaze,
That I did judge your empire here
Was not of love alone but fear.

But as all that is violent
Doth by degrees relent ;
So when that fweeteft face,
Growing at laft to be fer'ene and clear,
    Did now appear
With all its wonted heav'nly grace,

And your appeased eyes did send
A beam from them so soft and mild
That former terrors were exil'd,
And all that could amaze did end ;
Darkness in me was chang'd to light,
Wonder to love, love to delight.

Nor here yet did your goodness cease
My heart and eyes to bless,
    For, being past all hope
That I could now enjoy a better state,
        An orient gate
(As if the Heav'ns themselves did ope)
First found in thee, and then disclos'd
    So gracious and sweet a smile,
That my soul ravished the while,
And wholly from itself unloos'd,
Seem'd hov'ring in your breath to rise
To feel an air of Paradise.

Nor here yet did your favours end,
For whilst I down did bend,
As one who now did miss
A soul which grown much happier than before
        Would turn no more,
You did bestow on me a kiss,

And in that kiſs a ſoul infuſe
Which was ſo faſhion'd by your mind,
And which was ſo much more refin'd
   Than that I formerly did uſe,
That if one ſoul found joys in thee,
The other framed them new in me.

But as thoſe bodies which diſpenſe
Their beams, in parting hence
Thoſe beams do recollect,
Until they in themſelves reſumed have
   The forms they gave;
So when your gracious aſpect
   From me was turned once away,   .
Neither could I thy ſoul retain
Nor you give mine leave to remain,
   To make with you a longer ſtay,
Or ſuffered ought elſe to appear
But your hair, night's hemiſphere.

Only as we in Loadſtones find
Virtue of ſuch a kind,
That what they once do give,
Being neither to be chang'd by any Clime
   Or forc'd by time,
Doth ever in its ſubjects live;

So though I be from you retir'd,
The power you gave yet ftill abides,
And my foul ever fo guides
By your magnetique touch infpir'd,
That all it moves, or is inclin'd,
Comes from the motions of your mind.

## A MERRY RIME

### SENT TO THE LADY WROTH UPON THE BIRTH OF MY LORD OF PEMBROKE'S CHILD, BORN IN THE SPRING.

MADAM, though I'm one of thofe,
    That every fpring ufe to compofe,
That is, add feet unto round profe,
Yet you a further art difclofe,
And can, as every body knows,
Add to thofe feet fine dainty toes.
Satyrs add nails, but they are fhrews.
My mufe therefore no further goes,
But for her feet craves fhooes and hofe,
Let a fair feafon add a Rofe.
While thus attir'd we'll oppofe
The tragick bufkins of our foes.
And herewith, Madam, I will clofe,
And 'tis no matter how it fhows:
All I care is, if the Child grows.

## THE THOUGHT.

IF you do love as well as I,
  Then every minute from your heart
    A thought doth part,
And winged with defire doth fly
Till it hath met in a ftreight line
    A thought of mine,
So like to yours, we cannot know
Whether of both doth come or go,
    Till we define
Which of us two that thought did owe.

I say then that your thoughts which pafs
Are not fo much the thoughts you meant
    As thofe I fent,
For as my image in a glafs
Belongs not to the glafs you fee,
    But unto me,
So when your fancy is fo clear
That you would think you faw me there,
    It needs muft be
That it was I did firft appear.

Likewife when I fend forth a thought
My reafon tells me, 'tis the fame
  Which from you came,
And which your beauteous Image wrought.
Thus while our thoughts by turns do lead
  None can precede ;
And thus while in each other's mind
Such interchanged forms we find,
  Our loves may plead
To be of more then vulgar kind.

May you then often think on me,
And by that thinking know 'tis true
  I thought on you.
I in the fame belief will be,
While by this mutual addrefs
  We will poffefs
A love muft live, when we do die.
Which rare and fecret property
  You will confefs,
If you do love as well as I.

## TO A LADY WHO DID SING
## EXCELLENTLY.

WHEN our rude and unfashioned words, that
    long
A being in their elements enjoy'd,
    Senfelefs and void,
Come at laft to be formed by thy tongue,
And from thy breath receive that life and place,
    And perfect grace,
That now thy power, diffuf'd through all their parts,
    Are able to remove
All the obftructions of the hardeft hearts,
And teach the moft unwilling how to love.

When they again, exalted by thy voice,
Tun'd by thy foul, difmifl'd into the air,
    To us repair,
A living, moving, and harmonious noife,
Able to give the love they do create
    A fecond ftate,

And charm not only all his griefs away,
   And his defects reſtore,
But make him perfect, who, the Poets ſay,
Made all was ever yet made heretofore.

When again all theſe rare perfections meet,
Compoſed in the circle of thy face,
   As in their place,
So to make up of all one perfect ſweet,
Who is not then ſo raviſhed with delight,
   Ev'n of thy ſight,
That he can be aſſur'd his ſenſe is true,
   Or that he die, or live,
Or that he do enjoy himſelf, or you,
Or only the delights, which you did give?

## MELANDER,

### SUPPOS'D TO LOVE SUSAN, BUT DID LOVE ANN.

WHO doth prefume my Miftrefs's name to fcan
    Goes about more than any way he can,
Since all men think that it is *Sufan.*   *Echo*—Anne.

What fayft ?  Then tell who is as white as Swan,
While others fet by her are pale and wan ;
Then, Echo, fpeak, Is it not *Sufan ?*  *Ec.*—Anne.

Tell, Echo, yet, who's Middle's but a fpan,
Some being grofs as bucket, round as pan ?
Say, Echo, then, Is it not *Sufan ?*  *Ec.*—Anne.

Say, is fhe not foft as meal without bran ?
Though yet in great haft once from me fhe ran,
Muft I not however love *Sufan ?*  *Ec.*—Anne.

## ECHO TO A ROCK.

THOU heaven-threatening Rock, gentler then
    fhe,
      Since of my pain
    Thou ftill more fenfible will be,
Only when thou giv'ft leave but to complain.
        *Echo*—Complain.
But thou doft anfwer too, although in vain.
Thou anfwer'ft when thou can'ft no pity fhow.
        *Echo*—Oh!
    What, canft thou fpeak and pity too?
    Then yet a further favour do,
And tell if of my griefs I any end fhall know.
        *Echo*—No.
Sure fhe will pity him that loves her fo truly.
        *Echo*—You lie.
Vile Rock, thou now grow'ft fo unruly,
That hadft thou life, as thou haft voice,
    Thou fhouldft die at my foot.
        *Echo*—Die at my foot.

Thou canft not make me do't
Unlefs thou leave it to my choice,
Who thy hard fentence fhall fulfill,
When thou fhalt fay I die to pleafe her only will.
    *Echo*—I will.
When fhe comes hither, then, I pray thee, tell
Thou art my Monument, and this my laft farewell.
    *Echo*—Well.

## ECHO IN A CHURCH.

WHEN ſhall my troubled ſoul at large
     Diſcharge
The burden of her ſins, oh where?
    *Echo*—Here.
Whence comes this voice I hear?
  Who doth this grace afford?
  If it be thou, O Lord,

Say if thou hear my prayers, when I call.
    *Echo*—All.
And wilt thou pity grant when I do cry?
    *Echo*—I.

Then though I fall,
    Thy grace will my defects ſupply.
But who will keep my ſoul from ill,
Quench bad deſires, reform my Will?
    *Echo*—I will.

## Echo in a Church.

O may that Will and Voice be bleſt
Which yields ſuch comforts unto one diſtreſt !
More bleſſed yet, would'ſt thou thyſelf unmaſk,
Or tell at leaſt who undertakes this taſk.
　　　　*Echo*—Aſk.

Since now with crying I am grown ſo weak,
I ſhall want force even to crave thy name.
O ſpeak before I wholly weary am.
　　　　*Echo*—I am.

# TO HIS MISTRESS FOR HER TRUE
# PICTURE.

DEATH, my life's Miſtreſs, and the Sovereign Queen
 Of all that ever breath'd, though yet unſeen,
My heart doth love you beſt, yet I confeſs,
Your picture I beheld, which doth expreſs
No ſuch eye-taking beauty; you ſeem lean,
Unleſs you're mended ſince.   Sure he did mean
No honour to you, that did draw you ſo;
Therefore I think it falſe.   Beſides, I know
The picture Nature drew (which ſure's the beſt)
Doth figure you by ſleep and ſweeteſt reſt.
Sleep, Nurſe of our life, Care's beſt repoſer,
Nature's high'ſt rapture, and the viſion giver.
Sleep, which when it doth ſeize us, ſouls go play,
And make Man equal as he was firſt day.
Yet ſome will ſay can pictures have more life
Than the original?   To end this ſtrife,
Sweet Miſtreſs come, and ſhew yourſelf to me
In your true form, while then I think to ſee
Some beauty Angelick, that comes to unlock
My body's priſon, and from life unfrock

My well-divorced Soul, and ſet it free
To liberty eternal : thus you ſee,
I find the Painter's error, and protect
Your abſent Beauties, ill drawn, by th'effect.
For grant it were your work and not the Grave's,
Draw Love by Madneſs then, Tyrants by Slaves,
Becauſe they make men ſuch.  Dear Miſtreſs, then,
If you would not be ſeen by owl-ey'd men,
Appear at noon i'th'Air, with ſo much light
The Sun may be a Moon, the Day a Night,
Clear to my ſoul, but dark'ning the weak ſenſe
Of thoſe, the other World's Cimmeriens,
And in your fatal robe embroidered
With Star characters, teaching me to read
The deſtiny of Mortals, while your clear brow
Preſents a Majeſty, to inſtruct me how
To love, or dread nought elſe : May your bright hair,
Which are the threads of life, fair crown'd appear,
With that your Crown of Immortality.
In your right hand, the Keys of Heaven be,
In th'other, thoſe of the Infernal Pit,
Whence none retires if once he enter it.
And here let me complain, how few are thoſe
Whoſe ſouls you ſhall from earth's vaſt dungeon looſe
To endleſs happineſs ; few that attend
You the true guide unto their journey's end.

75

And if old Virtue's way narrow were,
'Tis rugged now, having no paffenger.
Our life is but a dark and ftormy night,
To which fenfe yields a weak and glimmering light,
While wandering Man thinks he difcerneth all
By that which makes him but miftake and fall.
He fees enough, who doth his darknefs fee.
Thefe are great lights, by which lefs dark'ned be.
Shine then Sun-bright, or through my fenfes' veil,
A day ftar of the light doth never fail.
Shew me that goodnefs which compounds the ftrife
'Twixt a long ficknefs and a weary life;
Set forth that Juftice which keeps all in awe
Certain and equal more than any Law;
Figure that happy and eternal Reft,
Which till man do enjoy, he is not bleft;
Come and appear then, dear Soul-ravifher,
Heav'ns lighteft Ufher, Man's deliverer;
And do not think, when I new beauties fee,
They can withdraw my fettled love from thee.
Flefh-beauty ftrikes me not at all, I know:
When thou do'ft leave them to the grave, they fhow
Worfe than they now fhow thee: they fhall not move
In me the leaft part of delight, or love,
But as they teach your power. Be the nut brown,
The lovelieft colour which the flefh doth crown,

I'll think it like a Nut—a fair outfide,
Within which worms and rottennefs abide ;
If fair, then like the Worm itfelf to be ;
If painted, like their flime and fluttery.
If any yet will think their beauties beft,
And will againft you, fpite of all, conteft,
Seize them with Age; fo in themfelves they'll hate
What they fcorn'd in your picture, and too late
See their fault, and the Painter's.  Yet if this,
Which their great'ft plague and wrinkled torture is,
Pleafe not, you may to the more wicked fort,
Or fuch as of your praifes make a fport,
Denounce an open war, fend chofen bands
Of Worms, your foldiers, to their faireft hands,
And make them leprous, fcabb'd : upon their face
Let thofe your Pioneers, Ringworms, take their place,
And fafely near with ftrong approaches got,
Intrench it round, while their teeths' rampire rot,
With other Worms, nay with a damp inbred,
Sink to their fenfes, which they fhall not dread.
And thus may all that ere they prided in,
Confound them now.  As for the parts within
Send great Worms, which may undermine a way
Into their vital parts, and fo difplay
That, your pàle enfign on the walls; then let
Thofe worms your Veterans which never yet

77

Did fail, enter pell-mell and ranfack all.
Juft as they fee the well-rais'd building fall.
While they do this, your Forragers command,
The Caterpillars, to devour their land,
And with them Wafps, your wing'd-worm-horfemen, bring
To charge, in troop, thofe Rebels, with their fting.
All this, unlefs your beauty they confefs.

And now, fweet Miftrefs, let me awhile digrefs
To admire thefe noble Worms whom I invoke,
And not the Mufes.   You that eat through oak
And bark, will you fpare Paper and my Verfe,
Becaufe your praifes they do here rehearfe?

Brave Legions then, fprung from the mighty race
Of man corrupted, and which hold the place
Of his undoubted iffue: you that are
Brain-born, Minerva-like, and, like her, war,
Well arm'd, complete, mail'd-jointed foldiers,
Whofe force Herculean links in pieces tears,
To you the vengeance of all Spill-bloods falls,
Beaft-eating Men, Men-eating cannibals,
Death privileg'd, were you in funder fmit,
You do not lofe your life, but double it.
Beft-framed types of the Immortal Soul,
Which in your felves, and in each part, are whole.

78

Laſt-living Creatures, heirs of all the earth,
For when all men are dead, it is your birth ;
When you die, your brave ſelf-killed General,
For nothing elſe can kill him, doth end all.
What vermine-breeding body then thinks ſcorn
His fleſh ſhould be by your brave fury torn ?
Willing, to you, this carcaſs I ſubmit,
A gift ſo free, I do not care for it,
Which yet you ſhall not take until I ſee
My Miſtreſs firſt reveal herſelf to me.

Meanwhile, Great Miſtreſs, whom my ſoul admires,
Grant me your true picture, who it deſires,
That he your matchleſs beauty might maintain,
'Gainſt all men that will quarrels entertain.
For a Fleſh-Miſtreſs, the worſt I can do
Is but to keep the way that leads to you,
And howſoever the event doth prove,
To have Revenge below, Reward above.
Hear, from my body's priſon, this my call,
Who from my mouth-grate and eye-window bawl.

## EPITAPH ON SIR PHILIP SIDNEY,

### LYING IN ST. PAUL'S WITHOUT A MONUMENT, TO BE FASTENED UPON THE CHURCH DOOR.

R EADER,—
　　Within this church Sir Philip Sidney lies,
　Nor is it fit that I ſhould more acquaint,
　　　　Leſt Superſtition riſe,
　　　　And men adore,
　Soldiers, their Martyr; Lovers, their Saint.

## EPITAPH FOR HIMSELF.

R EADER,—
    The Monument which thou beholdeſt here,
    Preſents Edward Lord Herbert to thy ſight,
A man, who was ſo free from either hope or fear,
    To have, or loſe this ordinary light,
That when to elements his body turned were
    He knew, that as thoſe elements would fight,
So his Immortal Soul ſhould find above
With his Creator, Peace, Joy, Faith, and Love.

## SONNET.

YOU well-compacted groves, whofe light and fhade
    Mixt equally, produce nor heat nor cold,
Either to burn the young, or freeze the old,
But to one even temper being made,
Upon a Grove embroidering through each glade
An Airy Silver, and a Sunny Gold,
So clothe the pooreft that they do behold
Themfelves in riches which can never fade,
While the wind whiftles, and the birds do fing,
While your twigs clip, and while the leaves do frifs,
While the fruit ripens which thofe trunks do bring,
Senfelefs to all but love, do you not fpring
Pleafure of fuch a kind, as truly is
A felf renewing vegetable blifs?

*Made upon the Groves near Merlou Caftle.*

## TO THE C. OF D.*

SINCE in your face, as in a beauteous fphere,
    Delight and ftate fo fweetly mix'd appear,
That Love's not light, nor Gravity fevere,
All your attractive graces feem to draw,
A modeft rigor keepeth fo in awe,
That in their turns, each of them gives the law.

Therefore, though chafte and virtuous, defire
Through that, your native mildnefs, may afpire,
Until a juft regard it doft acquire ;
Yet if Love thence a forward hope project
You can, by virtue of a fweet neglect,
Convert it ftreight to reverend refpect.

Thus, as in your rare temper, we may find
An excellence fo perfect in each kind,
That a fair body hath a fairer mind ;
So all the beams you diverfly do dart,
As well on th'underftanding as the heart,
Of love and honour equal caufe impart.

---

* Poffibly the Countefs of Denbigh, the patronefs of Carew.

## DITTY.

### 1.

WHY doft thou hate return inftead of love?
  And with fuch mercilefs defpite
  My faith and hope requite?
Oh ! if th'affeftion cannot move,
Learn innocence yet of the Dove,
And thy difdain to jufter bounds confine.
Or if t'wards Man thou equally decline
The rules of Juftice and of Mercy too,
Thou may'ft thy love to fuch a point refine
As it will kill more than thy hate can do.

### 2.

Love, love, Melaina, then, though death enfue,
  Yet it is a greater fate
  To die through love than hate.
  Rather a viftory purfue
  To Beauty's lawful conqueft due,

Than tyrant eyes envenom with difdain.
Or if thy Power thou wouldft fo maintain
As equally to be both lov'd and dread,
Let timely Kiffes call to life again
Him whom thine eyes have Planet-ftrucken dead.

### 3.

Kifs, kifs, Melaina, then, and do not ftay
    Until thefe fad effects appear
    Which now draw on fo near,
    That didft thou longer help delay
    My foul muft fly fo faft away
As would at once both life and love divorce ;
Or if I needs muft die without remorfe,
Kifs and embalm me fo with that fweet breath,
That while thou triumph'ft o'er Love and his force,
I may triumph yet over Fate and Death.

## ELEGY FOR DOCTOR DUNN.*

WHAT though the vulgar and received praife
  With which each common Poet ftrives to raife
His worthlefs Patron, feem to give the height
Of a true excellence, yet as the weight
Forced from his centre, muft again recoil,
So every praife, as if it took fome foil
Only becaufe it was not well imploy'd,
Turns to thofe fenfelefs principles and void,
Which in fome broken fyllables being vouched
Cannot above an Alphabet be couched,
In which diffolved ftate they ufed to reft
Until fome other in new forms inveft
Their eafy matter, ftriving fo to fix
Glory with words and make the parts to mix.

But fince praife that wants truth, like words that want
Their proper meaning, doth it felf recant;
Such terms, however elevate and high,
Are but like meteors, which the pregnant Sky

---

* He will be better recognifed as Dr. John Donne. He
died March 31ft, 1631.

Varies in divers figures, till at laſt
They either be by ſome dark cloud o'recaſt,
Or wanting inward ſuſtence do devolve,
And into their firſt Elements reſolve.
Praiſes, like garments then, if looſe and wide,
Are ſubjeᶜt to fall off; if gay and pied,
Make men ridiculous : The juſt and grave
Are thoſe alone which men may wear and have.

How fitting were it then each had that part
Which is their due, and that no fraudulent art
Could ſo diſguiſe the truth but they might own
Their rights, and by that property be known.
For ſince Praiſe is publick inheritance,
If any Inter-Commoner do chance
To give or take more praiſe than doth belong
Unto his part, he doth ſo great a wrong,
That all who claim an equal intereſt
May him implead until he do deveſt
His uſurpations, and again reſtore
Unto the Publick what was theirs before.

Praiſes ſhould then, like definitions, be
Round, neat, convertible, ſuch as agree
To perſons, ſo that were their names conceal'd
Muſt make them known as well as if reveal'd,

Such as contain the kind and difference
And all the properties arifing thence.
All praifes elfe, as more or lefs than due,
Will prove, or ftrangly falfe, or weakly true.

Having delivered now what praifes are,
It refts that I fhould to the world declare
Thy praifes, DUNN, whom I fo lov'd alive
That with my witty Carew I fhould ftrive
To celebrate the dead, did I not need
A language by itfelf, which fhould exceed
All thofe which are in ufe : For while I take
Thofe common words, which men may even rake
From Dunghill-wits, I find them fo defiled,
Slubber'd and falfe, as if they had exiled
Truth and propriety, fuch as do tell
So little other things, they hardly fpell
Their proper meaning, and therefore unfit
To blazon forth thy merits, or thy wit.

Nor will it ferve that thou didft fo refine
Matter with words that both did feem divine
When thy breath utter'd them, for thou being gone
They ftreight did follow thee.   Let therefore none
Hope to find out an Idiom and Senfe
Equal to thee and to thy Eminence,

Unlcſs our gracious King give words their bound,
Call in falſe titles which each where are found
In Proſe and Verſe, and as bad Coin and Light
Suppreſs them and their values, till the right
Take place and do appear, and then in lieu
Of thoſe forg'd Attributes ſtamp ſome anew,
Which being current and by all allow'd
In Epitaphs and Tombs might be avow'd
More then their Eſcucheons.   Meanwhile, becauſe
Nor praiſe is yet confined to its laws,
Nor railing wants his proper dialcɕt,
Let thy detraɕtion thy late life deteɕt,
And though they term all thy heat, forwardneſs,
Thy ſolitude, ſelf-pride, faſts, niggardneſs,
And on this falſe ſuppoſal would infer
They teach not others right, themſelves who err,
Yet as men to the adverſe part do ply
Thoſe crooked things, which they would reɕtify,
So would perchance to looſe and wanton Man
Such vice avail more than their virtues can.

## THE BROWN BEAUTY.

### 1.

WHILE the two contraries of Black and White,
    In the Brown Fay are ſo well unite,
That they no longer now ſeem oppoſite,
Who doubts but love hath this his colour choſe,
Since he therein doth both th'extremes compoſe,
And as within their proper Centre cloſe ?

### 2.

Therefore, as it preſents not to the view
That whitely raw and unconcocted hue
Which, Beauty, Northern Nations think the true,
So neither hath it that aduſt aſpect
The Moor and Indian ſo much affect,
That for it they all other do reject.

### 3.

Thus while the White well ſhadow'd doth appear,
And black doth through his luſtre grow ſo clear
That each in other equal part doth bear,

All in fo rare proportion is combin'd
That the fair temper, which adorns her mind,
Is even to her outward form confin'd.

4.

Fay, your fexe's honour, then fo live
That when the world fhall with contention ftrive
To whom they would a chief perfection give,
They might the controverfy fo decide
As, quitting all extremes on either fide,
You more than any may be dignify'd.

## AN ODE

### UPON A QUESTION MOVED WHETHER LOVE SHOULD CONTINUE FOR EVER.

HAVING interr'd her Infant-birth,
    The wat'ry ground, that late did mourn
Was ftrew'd with flow'rs, for the return
    Of the wifh'd Bridegroom of the Earth.

The well-accorded Birds did fing
    Their hymns unto the pleafant time,
    And in a fweet conforted chime
Did welcome in the cheerful Spring.

To which, foft whiftles of the Wind,
    And warbling murmurs of a Brook,
    And varied notes of leaves that fhook,
An harmony of parts did bind.

While doubling joy unto each other
    All in fo rare confent was fhown,
    No happinefs that came alone,
Nor pleafure that was not another.

When with a love none can exprefs
  That mutually happy pair,
  Melander and Celinda fair,
The feafon with their loves did blefs.

Walking thus towards a pleafant grove,
  Which did, it feem'd, in new delight
  The pleafures of the time unite,
They give a triumph to their love.

They ftay'd at laft and on the grafs
  Repofed fo, as o're his breaft
  She bow'd her gracious head to reft,
Such a weight as no burden was.

While over either's compafs'd waift
  Their folded arms were fo compof'd
  As if in ftraiteft bonds inclof'd,
They fuffer'd for joys they did tafte.

Long their fixt eyes to Heaven bent,
  Unchanged they did never move,
  As if fo great and pure a love
No glafs but it could reprefent.

When, with a fweet though troubled look,
  She firft brake filence, faying, Dear Friend,
  O that our love might take no end,
Or never had beginning took!

93

I fpeak not this with a falfe heart
   (Wherewith his hand fhe gently ftrain'd),
   Or that would change a love maintain'd
With fo much faith on either part;

Nay, I proteft; though Death with his
   Worft Counfel fhould divide us here,
   His terrors could not make me fear
To come where your lov'd prefence is.

Only, if love's fire with the breath
   Of life be kindled, I doubt
   With our laft air 'twill be breath'd out,
And quenched with the cold of death;

That if affection be a line
   Which is clof'd up in our laft hour,
   Oh, how 'twould grieve me, any pow'r
Could force fo dear a love as mine!

She fcarce had done, when his fhut eyes
   An inward joy did reprefent
   To hear Celinda thus intent
To a love he fo much did prize,

Then with a look, it feem'd deny'd
   All earthly pow'r but hers, yet fo
   As if to her breath he did owe
This borrow'd life, he thus replied:

O you, wherein, they fay, Souls reft
   Till they defcend, pure heavenly fires,
   Shall luftful and corrupt defires
With your immortal feed be bleft ?

And fhall our Love, fo far beyond
   That low and dying appetite,
   And which fo chaft defires unite,
Not hold in an eternal bond ?

It is, becaufe we fhould decline,
   And wholly from our thoughts exclude
   Objects that may the fenfe delude
And ftudy only the Divine.

No fure, for if none can afcend
   Ev'n to the vifible degree
   Of things created, how fhould we
The invifible comprehend ?

Or rather, fince that Pow'r expreft
   His greatnefs in his works alone,
   Being here beft in's Creatures known,
Why is he not lov'd in them beft ?

But is't not true, which you pretend,
   That fince our love and knowledge here,
   Only as parts of life appear,
So they with it fhould take their end ?

# An Ode.

O no, Belov'd, I am moſt ſure
   Thoſe vertuous habits we acquire
   As being with the Soul entire
Muſt with it evermore endure ;

For if, where ſins and vice reſide
   We find ſo foul a guilt remain,
   As never dying in his ſtain
Still puniſh'd in the Soul doth bide ;

Much more that true and real joy,
   Which in a virtuous love is found
   Muſt be more ſolid in its ground
Then Fate or Death can e're deſtroy.

Elſe ſhould our Souls in vain elect,
   And vainer yet were Heaven's laws,
   When to an everlaſting Cauſe
They gave a periſhing effect.

Nor here on earth then, or above,
   Our good affection can impair,
   For where God doth admit the fair
Think you that he excludeth Love ?

Theſe eyes again then eyes ſhall ſee,
   And hands again theſe hands enfold,
   And all chaſte pleaſures can be told
Shall with us everlaſting be.

For if no ufe of fenfe remain,
    When bodies once this life forfake,
    Or they could no delight partake,
Why fhould they ever rife again ?

And if every imperfect mind
    Make love the end of knowledge here,
    How perfect will our love be, where
All imperfection is refined !

Let then no doubt, Celinda, touch,
    Much lefs your faireft mind invade :
    Were not our fouls immortal made
Our equal loves can make them fuch.

So when one wing can make no way
    Two joined can themfelves dilate,
    So can two perfons propagate
When fingly either would decay.

So when from hence we fhall be gone,
    And be no more, nor you, nor I,
    As one another's myftery,
Each fhall be both, yet both but one.

This faid, in her uplifted face,
    Her eyes, which did that beauty crown,
    Were like two ftars, that having fall'n down,
Look up again to find their place.

While fuch a movelefs filent peace
   Did ceafe on their becalmed fenfe,
   One would have thought fome Influence
Their ravifh'd fpirits did poffefs.

## THE GREEN-SICKNESS BEAUTY.

THOUGH the pale white within your check
        compof'd,
And doubtful light unto your eye confin'd,
Though your fhort breath not from it felf unloof'd,
And carelefs motions of your equal mind,
Argue your beauties are not all difclof'd,

Yet as a rifing beam, when firft 'tis fhewn,
Points fairer, than when it afcends more red,
Or as a budding rofe, when firft 'tis blown,
Smells fweeter far, than when it is more fpread
As all things beft by principles are known,

So in your green and flourifhing eftate
A beauty is difcern'd more worthy love
Than that which further doth itfelf dilate,
And thofe degrees of variation prove,
Our vulgar wits fo much do celebrate.

Thus though your eyes dart not that piercing blaze,
Which doth in bufy Lovers' looks appear,
It is becaufe you do not need to gaze
On other objects than your proper fphere,
Nor wander further than to run that maze.

So, if you want that blood which muft fucceed,
And give at laft a tincture to your fkin,
It is, becaufe neither in outward deed,
Nor inward thought, you yet admit that fin,
For which your cheeks a guilty blufh fhould need.

So if your breath do not fo freely flow,
It is becaufe you love not to confume
That vital treafure, which you do beftow
As well to vegetate as to perfume
Your Virgin leaves, as faft as they do grow.

Yet ftay not here.  Love for his right will call:
You were not born to ferve your only will,
Nor can your beauty be perpetual.
'Tis your perfection for to ripen ftill,
And to be gathered, rather than to fall.

## THE GREEN-SICKNESS BEAUTY.

FROM thy pale look, while angry Love doth feem
   With more imperioufnefs to give his Law
Than when he blufhingly doth beg efteem,
   We may obferve pied beauty in fuch awe,
That the brav'ft colour under her command
   Affrighted, oft before you doth retire,
While, like a Statue of your felf, you ftand
   In fuch symmetrique form, as doth require
No luftre but his own : As then in vain
   One fhould flefh-colouring to ftatues add,
So were it to your native White a Stain,
   If it in other ornaments were clad,
Than what your rich proportions do give,
   Which in a boundlefs fair being unconfin'd,
Exalted in your foul, fo feem to live,
   That they become an emblem of your mind,
That fo, who to your Orient White fhould join
   Thofe fading qualities moft eyes adore,
Were but like one, who gilding Silver Coin,
   Gave but occafion to fufpect it more.

## LA GRALLETTA GALLANTE,

### OR

### THE SUN-BURN'D EXOTIQUE BEAUTY.

**I.**

CHILD of the Sun, in whom his Rays appear
  Hatch'd to that luftre, as doth make thee wear
Heavn's livery in thy fkin, what need'ft thou fear
The injury of Air, and change of Clime,
When thy exalted form is fo fublime
As to tranfcend all power of change or time?

**2.**

How proud are they that in their hair but fhow
Some part of thee, thinking therein they owe
The greateft beauty Nature can beftow,
When thou art fo much fairer to the fight,
As beams each where diffufed are more bright
Than their deriv'd and fecondary light.

### 3.

But Thou art cordial both to fight and tafte,
While each rare fruit feems in his time to hafte
To ripen in thee, till at length they wafte
Themfelves to inward fweets, from whence again,
They, like Elixirs, paffing through each vein,
An endlefs circulation do maintain.

### 4.

How poor are they then, whom if we but greet,
Think that raw juice, which in their lips we meet,
Enough to make us hold their Kiffes fweet;
When that rich odour, which in thee is fmelt,
Can it felf to a balmy liquor melt,
And make it to our inward fenfes felt.

### 5.

Leave then thy Country, Soil, and Mother's Home,
Wander a Planet this way, till thou come
To give our Lovers here their fatal doom,
While, if our beauties fcorn to envy thine,
It will be juft they to a Jaundice pine,
And by thy Gold, fhow like fome Copper-Mine.

## PLATONICK LOVE.

### 1.

MADAM, your beauty and your lovely parts
    Would fcarce admit poetic praife and arts,
As they are Love's moft fharp and piercing darts;
Though, as again they only wound and kill,
The more deprav'd affections of our will,
You claim a right to commendation ftill.

### 2.

For as you can unto that height refine
All Loves delights, as while they do incline
Unto no vice, they fo become divine,
We may as well attain your excellence,
As, without help of any outward fenfe
Would make us grow a pure Intelligence.

### 3.

And as a Soul, thus being quite abſtraƈt,
Complies not properly with any aƈt,
Which from its better Being may detraƈt,
So, through the virtuous habits which you infuſe
It is enough that we may like and chooſe,
Without preſuming yet to take or uſe.

### 4.

Thus Angels in their ſtarry Orbs proceed
Unto Affeƈtion, without other need
Than that they ſtill on contemplation feed,
Though as they may unto this Orb deſcend,
You can, when you would ſo much lower bend,
Give Joys beyond what Man can comprehend.

### 5.

Do not refuſe, then Madam, to appear,
Since every radiant Beam comes from your Sphere,
Can ſo much more than any elſe endear,
As while through them we do diſcern each Grace
The multiplied lights from every Place,
Will turn and circle, with their rays, your face.

## PLATONICK LOVE.

### 1.

MADAM, believe't, Love is not fuch a toy,
As it is fport but for the Idle Boy,
Or wanton Youth, fince it can entertain
Our ferious thoughts, and make us know how vain
All time is fpent we do not thus imploy.

### 2.

For though ftrong paffion oft on youth doth feize
It is not yet affection, but difeafe ;
Caufed from repletion, which their blood doth vex,
So that they love not Woman, but the Sex,
And care no more than how themfelves to pleafe.

### 3.

Whereas true Lovers check that appetite
Which would prefume further than to invite
The Soul unto that part it ought to take,
When that from this addrefs it would but make
Some introduction only to delight.

4.

For while they from the outward fenfe tranfplant
The love grew there in earthly mould, and fcant,
To the Soul's fpacious and immortal field,
They fpring a love eternal, which will yield
All that a pure affection can grant.

5.

Befides, what time or diftance might effect
Is thus remov'd, while they themfelves connect
So far above all change, as to exclude
Not only all which might their fenfe delude,
But mind to any object elfe effect.

6.

Nor will the proof of Conftancy be hard
When they have plac'd upon their Mind that guard
As no ignoble thought can enter there,
And Love doth fuch a Virtue perfevere,
And in it felf fo find a juft reward.

7.

And thus a love, made from a worthy choice,
Will to that union come, as but one voice,
Shall fpeak, one thought but think the other's will,
And while, but frailty, they can know no ill,
Their fouls more than their bodies muft rejoice.

### 8.

In which eftate nothing can fo fulfill
Thofe heights of pleafure, which their fouls inftill
Unto each other, but that love thence draws
New Arguments of joy, while the fame caufe
That makes them happy, makes them greater ftill.

### 9.

So that however multiplied and vaft
Their love increafe, they will not think it paft
The bounds of growth, till their exalted fire
Being equally inlarg'd with their defire,
Transform and fix them to one Star at laft.

### 10.

Or when that otherwife they were inclin'd
Unto thofe publick joys, which are affign'd
To blelfed Souls when they depart from hence,
They would, befides what Heaven doth difpenfe,
Have their contents they in each other find.

# THE IDEA,

## MADE OF ALNWICK IN HIS EXPEDITION TO SCOTLAND WITH THE ARMY, 1639.

ALL Beauties vulgar eyes on earth do fee,
　　At beft but fome Imperfect Copies be
Of thofe the Heavens did at firft decree ;

For though th' Ideas of each fev'ral kind
Conceiv'd above by the Eternal Mind
Are fuch, as none can error in them find,

Since from his thoughts and prefence he doth bar
And fhut out all deformity fo far,
That the leaft beauty near him is a Star.

As Nature yet from far th' Ideas views,
And doth befides but vile materials choofe,
We in her works obferve no fmall abufe.

Some of her figures therefore foil'd and blurr'd,
Show as if Heaven had no way concurr'd
In fhapes fo difproportion'd and abfurd.

Which being again vex'd with fome hate and fpite
That doth in them vengeance and rage excite,
Seem to be tortur'd and deformed quite.

While fo being fixt, they yet in them contain
Another fort of uglinefs and ftain,
Being with old wrinkles interlin'd again.

Laftly, as if Nature ev'n did not know
What colour every fev'ral part fhould owe,
They look as if their Galls would overflow.

Fair is the Mark of Good, and Foul, of ill,
Although not fo infallibly, but ftill
The proof depends moft on the mind and will.

As Good yet rarely in the Foul is met,
So 'twould as little by its union get,
As a rich Jewel that were poorly fet.

For fince Good firft did at the Fair begin,
Foul being but a punifhment for fin,
Fair's the true outfide to the Good within.

In thefe the Supreme Pow'r then fo doth guide
Nature's weak hand, as he doth add befide
All by which Creatures can be dignified,

While you in them fee fo exact a line,
That through each fev'ral parts a glimpfe doth fhine
Of their original and form divine.

Therefore the characters of fair and good
Are fo fet forth, and printed in their blood,
As each in other may be underftood.

That Beauty fo accompanied with Grace,
And equally confpicuous in the face,
In a fair Woman's outfide takes the place.

Thus while in her all rare perfection meets,
Each, as with Joy, its fellow beauty greets,
And varies fo into a thoufand fweets.

Or if fome tempting thought do fo affault
As doubtful fhe 'twixt two opinions halt,
A gentle blufh corrects and mends the fault.

That fo fhe ftill fairer, and better grows,
Without that thus fhe more to paffion owes
Than what frefh colour on her cheeks beftows.

To which again her lips fuch helps can add
As both will chafe all grievous thoughts and fad,
And give what elfe can make her good or glad.

# The Idea.

As Statuaries, yet having fram'd in Clay
An hollow image, afterwards convey
The molten metal through each feveral way,

But when it once unto its place hath paft,
And th'inward Statua perfectly is caft,
Do throw away the outward Clay at laft.

So when that form the Heavns at firft decreed
Is finifhed within, Souls do not need
Their Bodies more, but would from them be freed.

For who ftill cover'd with their earth would lie?
Who would not fhake their fetters off and fly,
And be at leaft, next to a Deity?

However then you be moft lovely here,
Yet, when you from all Elements are clear,
You far more pure and glorious fhall appear.

Thus from above I doubt not to behold
Your fecond felf renew'd in your own mold,
And rifing thence fairer then can be told.

From whence afcending to the Elect and Bleft
In your true Joys you will not find it leaft
That I in Heav'n fhall know, and love you beft.

For while I do your coming there attend,
I ſhall much time on your Idea ſpend,
And note how far you all others tranſcend.

And thus, though you more than an angel be,
Since being here to Sin and Miſchief free,
You will have raiſ'd your ſelf to their degree,

That ſo, victorious over Death and Fate,
And happy in your everlaſting ſtate,
You ſhall triumphant enter Heaven gate.

Haſten not thither yet, for as you are
A Beauty upon Earth without compare,
You will ſhew beſt ſtill where you are moſt rare.

Live all our lives then ; If the picture can
Here entertain a loving abſent Man,
Much more the Idea whence you firſt began.

## PLATONICK LOVE.

DISCONSOLATE and fad,
　　So little hope of remedy I find
That when my matchlefs Miftrefs were inclin'd
To pity me, 'twould fcarcely make me glad,
The difcompofing of fo fair a mind
Being that which would to my Afflictions add.

　　For when fhe fhould repent,
This Act of Charity had made her part
With fuch a precious Jewel as her Heart,
Might fhe not grieve that e'er fhe did relent?
And then were it fit I felt the fmart
Until I grew the greateft penitent.

　　Nor were't a good excufe,
When fhe pleaf'd to call for her Heart again,
To tell her of my fuffering and pain,
Since that I fhould her Clemency abufe,
While fhe did fee what wrong fhe did fuftain,
In giving what fhe juftly might refufe.

Vex'd thus with me at laft,
When from her kind reftraint fhe now were gone,
And I left to the Manacles alone,
Should I not on another Rock be caft?
Since they who have not yet content, do moan
Far lefs than they whofe hope thereof is paft?

Befides I would deferve,
And not live poorly on the alms of Love,
Or claim a favour did not fingly move
From my regard: if fhe her joys referve
Unto fome other, fhe at length fhould prove,
Rather than beg her pity I would ftarve.

Let her then be ferene,
Alike exempt from pity and from hate,
Let her ftill keep her dignity and ftate,
Yet from her glories fomething I fhall glean,
For when fhe doth them everywhere dilate
A beam or two to me muft intervene.

And this fhall me fuftain,
For though due merit I cannot exprefs,
Yet fhe fhall know none ever lov'd for lefs
Or eafier reward. Let her remain
Still great and good, and from her Happinefs
My chief contentment I will entertain.

Reftrained hopes, though you dare not afpire
To fly an even pitch with my defire,
Yet fall no lower, and at leaft take heed
That you no way unto defpair proceed,
Since in what form fo'er you keep entire
I fhall the lefs all other comforts need.

I know how much prefumption did tranfcend,
When that affection could at moft pretend
To be believ'd, would needs yet higher foar
And love a Beauty which I fhould adore,
Though yet therein I had no other end,
But to affure that none could love her more.

Only may fhe not think her beauty lefs
That on low objects it doth ftill exprefs
An equal force, while it doth rule all hearts
Alike in the remot'ft as neareft parts,
Since if it did at any diftance ceafe
It wanted of that pow'r it fhould impart.

Small earthly lights but to fome fpace extend,
And then unto the dim and dark do tend,
And common heat doth at fome length fo ftop
That it cannot fo much as warm one drop,
While light and heat that doth from Heav'n defcend
Warms the low Valley more than the Mountain top.

Nor do they always beſt of the Heav'ns deſerve,
Who gaze on't moſt, but they who do reſerve
Themſelves to know it, ſince not all that will
Climb up into a Steeple or a Hill
So well its pow'r and influence obſerve,
As they who ſtudy and remark it ſtill.

Would ſhe then in full glory on me ſhine,
An Image of that Light which is divine,
I then ſhould ſee more clear, while ſhe did draw
Me upwards, and the vapors twixt us awe.
To open her eyes, were to open mine,
And teach her wonders which I never ſaw.

Nor would there thus be any cauſe to fear,
That while her pow'r attractive drew me near,
The odds betwixt us would the leſſer ſhow,
Since the moſt common Underſtandings know
That inequalities ſtill moſt appear,
When brought together and compoſed ſo.

As there is nothing yet doth ſo excell,
But there is found, if not its parallel,
Yet ſomething ſo conform, as though far leaſt
May yet obtain therein an Intereſt,
Why may not faith and truth then join ſo well
As they may ſuit her rare perfections beſt ?

Then, hope, fuſtain thy ſelf; though thou art hid
Thou liveſt ſtill, and muſt till ſhe forbid ;
For when ſhe would my vows and love rejeƈt,
They would a Being in themſelves projeƈt,
Since infinites as they, yet never did,
Nor could conclude without ſome good effeƈt.

# A MEDITATION

## UPON HIS WAX-CANDLE BURNING OUT.

WHILE thy ambitious flame doth ſtrive for height,
   Yet burneth down as clogged with the weight
Of earthly parts, to which thou art combin'd,
Thou ſtill doſt grow more ſhort of thy deſire,
And doſt in vain unto that place aſpire
   To which thy native powers ſeem inclin'd.

Yet when at laſt thou com'ſt to be diſſolv'd,
And to thy proper principles rèſolv'd,
   And all that made thee now is diſcompoſ'd,
Though all thy terreſtrial part in aſhes lies,
Thy more ſublime to higher Regions flies,
   The reſt being to the middle ways expoſ'd.

And while thou doeſt thy ſelf each where diſperſe
Some parts of thee make up this Univerſe,
   Others a kind of dignity obtain,
Since thy pure Wax, in its own flame conſum'd,
Volumes of incenſe sends, in which perfum'd
   Thy ſmoak mounts where thy fire could not attain.

More more our Souls then, when they go from hence,
And back unto the Elements difpenfe,
    All that built up our frail and earthly frame
Shall through each pore and paffage make their breach,
Till they with all their faculties do reach
    Unto that place from whence at firft they came.

Nor need they fear thus to be thought unkind
To thofe poor Carcafes they leave behind,
    Since being in unequal parts commix'd
Each in his Element their place will get;
And who thought Elements unhappy yet
    As long as they were in their ftations fix'd?

Or if they fally forth, is there not light
And heat in fome, and fpirit prone to fight?
    Keep they not in Earth and Air the field?
Befides, have they not pow'r to generate
When more than Meteors they Stars* create,
    Which while they laft, fcarce to the brighteft yield?

That fo in them we more than once may live,
While thefe materials which here did give
    Our bodies effence, and are moft of ufe,
Quick'ned again by the world's common foul,
Which in it felf and in each part is whole,
    Can various forms in divers kinds produce.

---

* In the Conftellation of Caffiopeia, 1572.

If, then, at worſt, this our condition be
When to themſelves the Elements are free,
   And each doth to its proper place revert,
What may we not hope from our part divine
Which can this droſs of Elements refine
   And them unto a better ſtate aſſert?

Or if as clods upon this earthly ſtage,
Which repreſents nothing but change or age,
   Our ſouls would all their burdens here diveſt,
They ſingly may that glorious ſtate acquire,
Which fills alone their infinite deſire
   To be of perfeſt happineſs poſſeſt.

And therefore I who do not live and move
By outward ſenſe ſo much as faith and love,
   Which is not in inferior Creatures found,
May unto ſome immortal ſtate pretend,.
Since by theſe wings I thither may aſcend
   Where faithful loving Souls with joys are crown'd

## OCTOBER 14, 1664.

ENRAGING Griefs, though you moſt divers be,
    In your firſt cauſes you may yet agree
To take an equal ſhare within my heart,
Since, if each grief ſtrive for the greateſt part,
You needs muſt vex yourſelves as well as me.


For your own ſakes and mine then make an end.
In vain you do about a Heart contend,
Which, though it ſeem in greatneſs to dilate,
Is but a tumor, which in this its ſtate
The choiceſt remedies would but offend.


Then ſtorm't at once.   I neither feel conſtraint,
Scorning your worſt, nor ſuffer any taint,
Dying by multitudes, though if you ſtrive,
I fear my heart may thus be kept alive,
Until it under its own burden faint.

What is't not done ? Why then my God, I find,
Would have me ufe you to reform my mind,
Since through his help I may from you extract
An effence pure, fo fpriteful and compact
As it will be from groffer parts refin'd.

Which being again converted by his grace
To godly forrow, I may both efface
Thofe fins firft cauf'd you, and together have
Your pow'r to kill turn'd to a pow'r to fave,
And bring my Soul to its defired place.

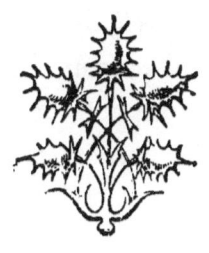

## *IN STATUAM LIGNEAM OVERBURII.*

CERNIS Overburi, non ære aut marmore, vultum
    Sed Ligno Hiberno dic, age, nonne placet ?

## *DE C. DE S.*

HÆC anima, ut fuerit terrenâ libera mole,
    Venerit et fummo confpicienda Deo,
Talibus et tantis vitiis fpurcata, trahetur,
    Haud dubium, ad pœnam fuppliciumque grave.
Viderit : at pulchrum dabitur cum fumere corpus,
    Eximium, credo, perdere nollet opus.

*EPITAPHIUM IN ANAGRAMMA NOMINIS SUI,*
## REDDOR UT HERBÆ.

QUAS turgens flos mane decet, quas aruit omnes
Una dies, quas morte cita, nova vita fequetur,
Non unquam moritura tamen, fic *Reddor ut Herbæ.*

## EPITAPH.
### IN SE ROMÆ FACTUM 1615.

VEROS ceu varios populi ridere timores
Expertus, vitæ melioris confcius, intus
Plaudebam, expectans faceret dum fabula finem.

## *IN TUMULUM DOMINI FRANCISCI*
## *VERE.*

ANGUSTUS nimis eft lapis pufillus,
    Vel, totum, foret ipfa terra, marmor ;
Angufta et fpolia et Trophæa ficta,
Hæc Belgæ tulerant, vel illa Iberi.
Cuncta angufta nimis videntur illi,
Qui victor toties mori volebat,
In fe poft alios, agens triumphum,
Ut dignum tumulum, Trophæa digna
Uni nil poterit referre vero.
Ni forte, ut maneat perenne nomen
Cui mundus fpolia, et caro triumphus,
Cælum fit Tumulus, Trophœa ftellæ.

## IN DIEM NATALITIUM,

### VIZ. 3 MAR.

VERE novo lux ufque redit quâ nafcor, at una
    Dum tempus redit, et fit numerofa dies,
Ver olim vires renovans, roburque recondens
Ætas fit tandem, triftis hyemfque mihi.

## FOR A DIAL.

DISCURRENS dubiæ, placidus compendia vitæ,
    Excipiens tacito gaudia tuta finu,
Præteritis lætare bonis, nec fæva futuri
Exagitet miferos cura premave dies.

Omnis in adverfum ruit hora, volatque retrorfum
    Et velut exhorrens jam peritura fugit.
Dum numerans delet, dumque addens fubtrahit, illa,
    Quæ vitæ ratio, calculus atque tuæ.

## IN ANSWER TO THE VERSES OF GUIET
### FOR THE PUCELLE D'ORLEANS, QUASI EXTEMPORE.

QUOD nequiere viri, potuit fi fœmina, quid ni
  Galle, fores tandem tu muliere minor?
Define, Galle, tuam tandem jactare Bubulcam,
  Seu Medæa fuit, five Medufa fuit.
Si canit ad Bellum, tamen eft Medæa vocanda,
  Carmina dum rauco concinit illa fono.
Hoftes fi cæfi, tamen eft dicenda Medufa,
  Dum nimis ad diræ virginis ora rigent.
Virgo fit tandem fed qualem nollet adulter,
  Seu Medæa fuit, five Medufa fuit.
Definat ergo fuam Gallus jactare *Johannam*,
  Saltem plena fuo non erit illa Deo.
Plena fuo vel nulla datur, vel Papa *Johanna*,
  Numine ; fit virgo quam licet illa minus.

## *IN ANSWER TO TILENUS*
### *WHEN I HAD THAT FATAL DEFLUXION IN MY HAND.*

QUÎ poſſim Phœbum ſuccenſum credere?
    Laudes
Quum facit ut ſcribas, Docte Tilene, meas.
Providus atque manum conſulto ſurripit iſtam
Ut melius poſſem nunc ſupereſſe tuâ.

## *DE HUGONE GROTIO,*
### *ARCÂ INCLUSO ET A CARCERE LIBERATO.*

CARCERE dum Carcer victus, Tenebriſque Tenebræ
    Vinclis cum demum vincla ſoluta tibi
Proſiliens mediâ tandem de mole, videris
Quidquid mortale eſt, depoſuiſſe ſimul.

## PRO LAUREATO POETA.

AT quorſum Juvenis, ſi nullo limine clauſus,
    Immiſtus canibus, ſaltuque vagatus in omni
Præcipites crebris damas latratibus urgens
Excurrit, ſecumque nihil non perdere tentat?
An mage grata viri tandem maturior ætas?
Qui furiis agitatus, atrox, atque omine triſti
Horrida funeſtis meditatur prælia campis? ¦
In propriam ſpeciemque ruens ita ſanguine gaudet
Conſeſſus ſatis, ut nullus ſibi concidat hoſtis.
Is potiorne domi qui futilis ambit honorem,
Inque leves populi gyros proclivis et auram,
Mercatur voces, falſâque cupidine tractus,
Incertam dubii ſectatur nominis umbram?
Heu fugias qui te fugiunt, et ferre recuſant
Imperium faſceſque tuos, quibus undique fauſtis
Candida ſupremos deſignant colla triumphos.
Sed ne nulla tibi demum victoria conſtet,
En prædam, formoſa, tuam, quam porrigit herba,
Et genua amplectens, ſeſe ultro dedere victam
Teſtatur, lauroque ſuâ tua tempora cingit.

Nec canos caufere meos (qui fymbola certa
Sunt fidei), tantâ folitum flammâve tremorem,
Immo nec errones tanquam, fed lumina fixa
Contemplare oculos tandem, neque bafia fpernas
Floridus ut defit color ori, fervat odorem,
Æmula paftillis fpirabunt labra rofatis
Bafia, mellito et fe lingua madore refolvet.
Denique feu noftro latitet nova pruna colore,
Nictet et implexus torvo fub lumine cautus
Arcitenens, mortis tandem feu fcena futuræ
Prodierim, vitam nobis dum dura negaris ;
Ah ! reddas faltem, nondum fatis arfit Amorem,
Cui fenium tempusve fidem cui præripit ullum.

## AD SERENISS. REGEM GUSTAVUM,

### A.D. 1631.

PER varios terræ tractus & diffita Regna,
  Inclyte Suedorum princeps, dum caftra movere
Conftituis, pacemque pio decernere bello,
Quæ te fecurum probitas, prudentia fortem,
Felicem virtus præftat, non omine vano
Fecit, ut antiquum Germania libera nomen
Accipiens rurfus fe jufto vindice tandem
Gaudeat, inque tuos fuccedat fponte triumphos.
Scilicet hoc potuit tua dextera fortis & ultrix,
Igneus atque vigor bello famiatus, & enfis
Quo ftricto late rutilanteque, fulgidus hoftes
Irruis in medios, denfam paffimque caternam
Difcutis, & longe percellis quæque timore,
Ut tibi nec fumi nubes glomerata, nec imo
Excuffus pulvis, pila nec confertior inftans
Obfcurare tuos validos, vel flectere, greffus
Poffint, è multo quin numine flamma corufcans
Perftringenfque oculos, infultus reddat inanes

Militis, innocuofque iǎus, ac irrita tela,
Dum tibi luftratæ cæcæ patuere tenebræ,
Inque tuam lucem caligo cedere vifa eft.
Inde citata tuum fequitur viǎoria curfum,
Inque gradus hæret certos figitque trophæa,
Aufpiciifque tuis illuftrior explicat alas ;
Queîs furfum veǎo, fuperas invifere fedes,
Inque novum tandem liceat tibi fidus abire
Clarius Arǎuri, et fufcæ jubar addere luci.

## EURYALE MŒRENS.

DEPRESSÆ valles piceis irriguæ fontibus,
    Herbæ marcidæ, cæca prætexentes Barathra,
Maligni colles hirfutis vepribus obfiti,
Afpera montium juga, exefis hiulca fpecubus,
Defrugatarum fegetum late patentia æquora,
Invifa Soli antra, confragofa præcipitia,
Abruptarum cautium nutantia undique cacumina,
Pendulæ taxi, cupreffis fuccrefcentes feralibus,
  Spelæorum inferna ducentium horrores facri,
Infauftæ ftryges, bubulantia ftygiæ avis omina,
Rauci ftridores, torvorum colla anguium fibila,
Prodigialium monftrorum exerta paffim capita,
Afpeçtus truces fiderum, diri portenta ætheris,
Vofque gementes umbræ, hic teftari liceat,
Nihil ufpiam fuiffe Euryale triftius.

1632

# MENSA LUSORIA;

## OR, A SHOVEL-BOARD-TABLE TO MR. MASTER.*

ROBORIS excelfi tabulatum fternitur ingens,
 Æquore productum levi, quod tramite recto
Procurrens, tandem quâ fe fubducit in imum
Diffecat exilis tranfverfim linea, fcena
Unde patet ludi, commiffo margine claufa,
Qui bini ternive notam certantibus aptat
Figitur extremo, feu preffus limite jactus,
Seu tremulus nutat, fibi nec conftare videtur.
Hic ubi conveniunt lufores, quifque monetam
Argento cufam, difci formâque nitentem
Librat in adverfam, quâ ducitur orbita, partem
Perpetuo jactu, fed quæ, fi forte feratur
Plus jufto, cadit in foveam, quæ limine fummo
Cernitur, at citra feptum fi tarda fatifcit,
Rejicitur jactus, totus fit & irritus inde.
Aft intra juftam datur ut confiftere metam
Promovet hic jactum, promotum dimovet ille.
Adjicit hic alium, fed quem depellere tentat
Nonnullus ; Nummos hic obfidet, impetit ille,
Obliquo Curfu : Multâ cadit ifte ruinâ,
Dum complexa fuo funduntur fingula nexu,
Et variata vices rerum fors undique verfat.
Ludere fic liceat manibus, fic ludere mufâ,
A ftudiis feffi quum jam deceffimus ambo.

---

* Thomas Mafter, "efteemed," fays Anthony Wood, "as a vast scholar, a general artift and linguift, a noted poet, and a moft florid preacher," was a fenior ftudent of Chrift Church. He affifted Herbert in collecting materials for the *Hiftory of Henry VIII.* He died in 1643.

## CHARISSIMO, DOCTISSIMO, JUCUNDISSIMOQUE JUXTIM AMICO
## THOMÆ MASTER.

*Hoc Epitaph. mœrens P. C. E. B. Herbert de Cherbury*, 1643.

QUI fis vel fueras, Amate Mafter,
    Lectorem fatis hæc docere poffunt;—
Quod terris fuit ut molefta vita,
Te dempto, mage fit molefta longe,
Quod Cœlum fuit ut beata fedes,
Auctum te, mage fit beata fedes.
In terris quid agis fide vacillans?
Si vita probus es, fruere, Lector,
Cœlo jam folito beatiore,
Mafter jam reliquis alacriore.
Vivat in æternum virtus ac diffita terræ
Luftret, ubique gravi fub Religione refurgens.

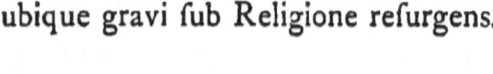

136